Between Love and Murder

Willow River Press
Between the Lines Publishing
410 Caribou Trail
Lutsen, MN 55612
btwnthelines.com

First Published: April 2020

Willow River Press is an imprint of Between the Lines Publishing.
The Liminal Books name and logo are trademarks of Between the Lines Publishing.

The publisher is not responsible for websites (or their content) that are not owned by the publisher.

ISBN: 978-1-950502-22-6 (paperback)
Printed in the United States

Between Love and Murder

Chris Bedell

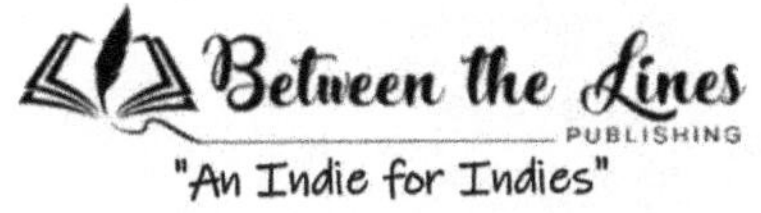

BEFORE

TUESDAY, SEPTEMBER 4, 2018

Expecting complete honesty was pointless.

Like with Santa Claus or the Tooth Fairy, or when a friend got a questionable haircut. Both the kid and friend could discover the truth without anyone playing the villain. Or like right now while I stood next to my locker in the school hallway. My best friend, Mallory, couldn't have said what she had. Yet I didn't have an ear wax problem, so the chances of her comment being misheard were slimmer than time travel happening.

I blinked. "Come again?"

She tugged at her backpack strap. "I'm sorry, Chad; I'm not trying to be awkward. I just couldn't lie anymore."

"Don't apologize for your feelings."

Telling her not to feel bad shouldn't have been the best response I came up with. Doing so only prolonged the inevitable: deciding about whether honesty or a fib was best. However, there was no right reaction to finding out Mallory had a crush on me. Some events—such as her revelation—couldn't be anticipated no matter how many A's I earned in school.

Mallory bit her lip. "We've been spending a lot of time together since July."

I chuckled. "We've always been close."

"Not since I started dating Tommy."

I scratched the side of my head. "What'd you expect to happen?"

She sighed. "To find out if you'd reciprocate."

Regardless of whether truthfulness was overemphasized, I couldn't deny how Mallory deserved a real answer. If roles were reversed, anger would've shot through my body if someone dangled something in front of me without any intention of following through.

"I don't feel the same way," I said.

She averted her gaze. "No worries."

"I need to know one thing."

"Sure," she said, still unable to make eye contact.

"Did I lead you on?" I asked.

"No. It's all me. I've been feeling lonely since July."

The high school's side-entrance door opened, and wind swooshed through the hallway. The MISSING poster fell off the wall, and my attention remained on the flier. Some truths couldn't be swallowed—like a teenager being here one minute and vanishing the next. Tragedies were supposed to be read about in the newspaper, not played out in real time in front of me.

She met my gaze after rubbing her eyes. "I can't stop thinking about Tommy."

"The police don't have any leads?"

"Nope."

Patting her shoulder might've been a natural gesture, yet I stopped myself. Even the smallest detail could be misunderstood, and I couldn't have that.

I gritted my teeth. "Have you spoken to his parents lately?"

She shrugged. "Even they've given up."

"I still think about Tommy too."

"You aren't mad at him?" Mallory asked.

"Dynamics change."

"Some things are unforgivable."

"People ditch people all the time for more popular friends."

"Doesn't make it fair. That was no way to start freshman year," Mallory said.

Mallory was right whether I admitted the truth to her or not. Just because I might not have constantly thought about the idea, didn't mean it wasn't correct. Cutting people off without a legitimate reason sucked. And in a way, empathy wasn't difficult. I might not have lost a boyfriend like Mallory had, yet the opportunity to one day reconnect with Tommy had been taken from me—at least in my imaginary alternative world where anything was possible.

"We can remain friends if you want," I said.

Mallory almost choked while more students flocked through the hallway and the chattering of numerous voices grew louder. "Absolutely," she said.

No offense to Mallory, but her response didn't inspire confidence. Not when a one-liner was all I had to hold onto.

"You don't hate me, do you?" Mallory asked.

Regardless of how her stomach might've been twisted in ten different directions, she should've had more confidence. It'd take a lot more than a crush to push me away. Besides, crushes were harmless 99.99% of the time. Liking someone who wouldn't reciprocate didn't mean the situation would resemble a scene from *Fatal Attraction*.

I waved my hand. "Don't be ridiculous."

"Good."

I forced a smile. "What's your first class?"

"I'm sorry, but I can't do this." Mallory darted away and was soon out of sight.

Maybe it was best for Mallory to have time to herself. Making the situation more awkward by forcing us to keep talking wouldn't help. Besides, distance might make Mallory realize the situation wasn't all bad. Just because the situation might've been the end of the world to her, didn't mean it was actually the end of the world.

Mallory's revelation was quite the way to start my first day of school, though. Handing in my AP US History summer homework and not having my teachers or guidance counselor mention college plans should've been my biggest challenge today.

Deep breaths. Empathizing with Mallory didn't mean having my pulse echo in my ear for the rest of the day. I had to live my life, and that was what I'd do.

So, I placed the notebooks I wouldn't need till later into my locker and clinked it shut. I then almost started shuffling down the hallway when a guy bumped into me and I fell onto the ground.

He laughed. "I'm sorry. I should've watched where I was going."

No shit. But no. Getting into a fight wasn't something I wanted to mention to Mom when she asked how my first day went. So, I sucked in a breath while counting to ten in my head.

He offered his hand, and I took it. I might not have wanted to start a brawl, yet at least he helped me. So, he might not have been the biggest turd in the world.

"Thanks," I said.

"Don't mention it."

I opened my mouth but couldn't speak. My heart even thumped faster. There was no denying how my gaze was fixated on this guy—whether it was his Henley tee-shirt, knee-ripped jeans and leather jacket, which gave him a slight edge, or his loafers. Good style was priceless.

He snorted. "Are you gonna say something, or are you just gonna stare?"

"I'm thinking…"

"Sure."

"I get distracted often," I said.

He smirked. "Take a picture. It lasts longer."

If I hadn't bit my lip when I first saw him, I had now. Bantering was one thing, yet he couldn't have mentioned taking a photo of him. Doing so reinforced how he might've been the arrogant guy I suspected he was.

"Can I get a name?" I asked.

"I'm Archie." He offered his hand again, and I shook it.

"I'm Chad."

"Nice to meet you." Archie ran his finger through his spiked hair while sunlight from a nearby window trickled into the hallway. It was almost as if his brown hair resembled a dishwasher blond shade because of the extra lighting.

"Same," I said.

A fruity and tangy scent wafted through air.

Okay. I'd have to get the name of whatever cologne Archie used—I never once met a guy who smelled so great. Or maybe I'd wait till our next chat. Mentioning his cologne during a subsequent conversation gave us something to discuss later.

He put his hands in his jacket pockets. "I just arrived in town last night, so I'm…"

"Nervous?" I interrupted.

Archie paused for a beat. "Yeah. Usually, I'm oozing with confidence."

I shook my finger at him. "Don't get cocky."

"Why? Is that a turnoff?"

I'd have to get a fake ID and buy a lotto ticket after school. "Turnoff" wasn't the same as complimenting someone on a new pair of shoes or losing weight. It reinforced the possibility of Archie flirting with me, even if I never once considered a guy that hot would give me attention.

"I'm a junior," he continued.

"Same."

He winked. "Wanna share any secrets about this school or town?"

"People aren't what they seem," I said.

"Boring. Even I could've figured that out."

"If you're the new kid, then does that mean you aren't seeing anyone?" I asked.

Pushing the boundaries of the conversation was harmless—I wouldn't say anything obscene. I just needed to see how far our talk would go.

Archie snickered. "Yeah, I'm single—no boyfriend or girlfriend."

Yup. I definitely had to buy a lotto ticket. It wasn't enough for him to flirt with me. He also had to maybe be bisexual like me, because even the most tolerant straight guy wouldn't have mentioned no boyfriend or girlfriend.

"I have to go to my locker, but we should hang one day after school." Archie patted my shoulder, and his hand lingered several seconds longer than it should have. Then, he was gone as fast as he appeared.

My mind should've been focused on how I wished I had the same confidence as Archie with tapping someone's shoulder. But no. My attention remained on the opposite end of the hallway. More specifically, Mallory. She continued staring at me, and my throat tightened.

Creepy. I would've expected Mallory to take more than five or ten minutes to get over our conversation. At a minimum, her face should've drooped, not have a hyena smile. Almost as if Mallory watched my entire conversation with Archie.

So, yeah. My back hairs remained up. I never once considered how Mallory was the lurking type.

AFTER

FRIDAY, DECEMBER 7, 2018

"We're making a mistake by going to the dance." I halted at a stop sign before turning right a few moments later, while the moon and stars illuminated the sky.

Mallory scoffed. "We don't have a choice."

Archie shifted his weight in the front passenger seat. "She has a point. The Snowflake Ball will be our alibi."

"Just focus on driving, Chad," Mallory said.

Leave it to me to get stuck driving us.

It wasn't enough for me to get dragged into the most fucked up situation of my life. Nope. I also had to be in charge of our transportation. I might not have said anything to Mallory and Archie, but the various thoughts weighing on my mind didn't make me the most stable driver.

I grunted. "How do we know you didn't plan for Tommy to die tonight?"

"Don't be ridiculous," Mallory said. "If I hadn't smacked him with the bookend, then you'd be dead."

I honked my horn at the driver in front of us. "You're the one who lied about everything."

"Now isn't the time to turn on each other," Mallory said.

I snorted. "That's rich. You made Archie break up with me because of feeling threatened."

"What was I supposed to do?" Mallory asked.

"You didn't have to blackmail Tommy to leave town on the Fourth of the July," I said.

Mallory grumbled. "How would you feel after discovering your boyfriend was sleeping with his sister?"

I slapped my cheeks after coming to another stop sign. Nope. I wasn't having a nightmare. Mallory had actually said it, even if I couldn't understand how Tommy and Gemma were sleeping together. That was the one thing most people agreed was immoral, yet socially acceptable behavior somehow escaped Tommy and Gemma.

"That's between Gemma and Tommy," I said.

"You didn't know how humiliating it was finding them in bed," Mallory said.

"But you recorded them having sex?" I asked.

Mallory screamed. "It ensured he'd leave town."

I nibbled on the inside of my lip before turning left. Somehow, Mallory wasn't wrong. Covering herself was smart since she was making such a big demand.

I would've saved my energy if I were Mallory, though. Nothing good came from thinking about a painful situation. If someone I dated pulled a stunt like Tommy had, then adios to that person.

"Except he blew through his trust fund and turned to you," I interrupted.

"Every plan has its flaws," Mallory said.

Funny way of putting it. If Mallory was smart enough to get Tommy and Gemma on tape, then she should've anticipated what she would've done if Tommy returned. Doing so was the least she could've done.

Archie pulled his seatbelt harder. "What's done is done."

"I'm more interested in knowing where his body is," Mallory said. "Tommy couldn't have disappeared into thin air."

Good question. Even I didn't fault Mallory for wondering why Tommy wasn't there when we got back to her house after cooling off in the woods. If we had his corpse, then we would've been in control of the situation.

Fuck. Corpse shouldn't have been in a seventeen-year-old's vocabulary. I was supposed to be concerned about the SAT's, doing well in school, and considering what colleges I wanted to apply to—not contemplating if I'd be arrested as an accessory.

"He seemed dead to me," I said.

"Maybe he was unconscious and walked away when we were in the woods," Mallory suggested.

"Then how did he escape?" I asked.

"Good point," Archie said.

"Were you really gonna let his parents and Gemma think Tommy was dead if he hadn't come back from Florida?" I asked.

"Don't mention that bitch," Mallory spat.

Mallory sure knew how to make me feel great. Both the tone and inflection in her voice made me feel happier than if a test was cancelled. NOT. If anything, I wanted to put a million miles between us. Nothing fun existed from realizing Mallory might've been more unhinged than the average teenager.

"What about his parents?" I demanded.

Only I'd make a comment about the parents. However, my mind couldn't help going there. Tommy might've been a jackass, but his parents didn't deserve to think he was dead if he were still alive. No parent deserved that; parents were supposed to die before their children—not after. And maybe, just maybe, my father's death was what made me empathetic. Even if Tommy's parents were a distraction we couldn't afford.

"They're just collateral damage," Mallory said.

Perhaps I didn't know Mallory as well as I thought. My best friend shouldn't have sounded more mechanical than a robot. Yet here I was, driving to the Snowflake Ball without a clue about how the situation would resolve itself.

"Tell me something," I said. "What was your plan for Tommy if you weren't gonna kill him?"

"I don't know. Maybe have Archie rough up him a little," Mallory said.

Archie titled his head towards Mallory. "You don't think your sister is involved?"

"Didn't you say she's chaperoning the dance?" I asked.

She nodded. "Yeah, Kelly's at the ball."

Archie shot me an apologetic look. "I'm sorry for breaking up with you."

Poor me. If only Archie's words could fix everything that happened between Mallory, him, and me over the last three months. But no. A well-meaning phrase couldn't wrap up the situation.

"I hope you're happy with yourself, Mallory," I said.

"Hardly," Mallory touted.

Archie massaged his forehead. "What are we gonna do if Tommy's body turns up?"

Criticizing Archie for his question would've meant also chastising myself. I would've been lying if I didn't acknowledge how Tommy's body lying on Mallory's living room floor one minute and gone the next confused me. That type of thing was only supposed to happen in movies, not real life.

"We'll deal with it later," Mallory said.

"Wow. You've got an answer for everything," I said.

Mallory shrieked, "If you hadn't come over to my house tonight, then you wouldn't be involved in this."

Damn her. She had to twist the situation so I was at fault. As if our lives weren't complicated enough at the moment.

"You're the whore who stole my boyfriend right as Archie and I were becoming a real couple," I said.

Yup. Mallory deserved to be insulted. My criticism wasn't based off her gender; it was based off fact. There was a right way and wrong way to behave, and quite often people did whatever the fuck they wanted without any consequences.

"You took him from me first," Mallory said.

"Not true. I had my eyes on him since the first day of school, whereas you wanted to hurt me because I didn't reciprocate your crush," I said.

"Please don't fight," Archie said. "There's obviously a lot of baggage, and we can sort it out later."

Somehow, my reason for being attracted to Archie escaped me. In this moment, he should've supported me, not Mallory. At least then I could've pretended everything would be fine between us.

Mallory snarled. "If you're looking for someone to blame, then blame Tommy. He brought the gun."

"Let's focus on pretending to enjoy the dance—it only takes one slip for everything to unravel," Archie said.

"You know what?" I said. "Did you ever consider you deserved Tommy's cheating?"

"You're insult would hold water if he hadn't been sleeping with Gemma long before we started dating," Mallory said.

I cackled. "Then that's it. Tommy must've been using you as a cover and never cared about you."

"You don't know that," Mallory quipped.

Archie continued rubbing his forehead. Whatever. Too bad for him, but I had no misgivings about my comment. Some people deserved every bad insult flung at them even though Mallory and I needed to shove our differences aside if we wanted to stay out of prison.

"I still don't understand why you agreed to help Mallory?" I asked, taking my eyes off the road for a beat.

Archie averted his gaze. "Mallory's fear of Tommy was the first time she was vulnerable with me."

"Don't talk about me—talk to me," Mallory said.

The clunky sound of my ignition halted a couple minutes after I parked in the high school parking lot. We exited the car, then a beeping sound echoed. I couldn't be too careful because of everything that happened this evening, so locking the car seemed most logical.

I exhaled a long breath. "Are we seriously gonna pretend nothing bad happened?"

"We don't have a choice," Mallory said.

Archie rubbed my shoulder. "It's only for a couple of hours."

"Let's get this over with," I said.

Mallory turned to me. "Just because I despise you, doesn't mean I think you're wrong. We'll eventually have to figure out what our story is gonna be going forward."

"We can worry about that later," Archie said.

How nice for Archie. I would've given anything for my jaw not to twitch. Stress just complicated life more and had zero positive benefits.

"How are we gonna do this?" I asked.

Mallory rolled her eyes. "What do you mean?"

The trees bobbed, and the wind nipped my face. Wow. Yet another reminder winter was fast approaching. In fact, it was a miracle the ground wasn't covered in snow.

"There are three of us," I said.

Mallory giggled. "Just like old times."

I glared at Mallory. "This isn't funny."

"What about tickets?" I asked.

"We don't need tickets if we have our school IDs," Mallory revealed.

Archie nodded. "Cool."

Mallory clicked her heels against the ground. "What are you waiting for?"

Archie looped one arm around Mallory's and the other around mine, then we trekked through the parking lot and towards the high school's main entrance. A burning sensation jabbed my stomach, though. Not labeling every situation was fair—labels weren't always all encompassing—yet this shouldn't have been my life. I was selfish enough to not want to share Archie with anyone. But here I was, in my own twisted thruple.

Whatever. My first step was making it through the rest of the evening—I'd worry about what would happen between us later. I could only deal with so many problems before my head exploded.

We turned the corner in the hallway after showing our ID's to one of the chaperones by the front entrance, only to cross paths with Dan and Rebecca.

Rebecca shook her head. "What are you three doing here?"

"Yeah." Dan rubbed a piece of lint off his blazer, yet my gaze should've been on his combed-back sandy blond hair. Apparently, Dan was capable of combing his hair, although I never once saw him put so much as gel in his hair before. "Having any drama is the last thing we want tonight."

"You didn't answer my question." Rebecca flipped her hair over her shoulders, accentuating her curls. Wow. Dan wasn't the only one capable of sprucing up his image because Rebecca had always worn her hair straight in all the years I had known her.

"It's complicated," I said.

Mallory gave me a look. "Keep your mouth shut, Chad."

Archie jabbed Mallory's shoulder. "Don't be mean."

Thank goodness Archie defended me. Disrespecting me was the last thing Mallory should've done. Any other person might've turned her into the police, yet I hadn't. Somehow, I convinced myself that our friendship was worth saving at some vague, distant point in the future.

Dan's eyes widened. "One of you better answer Rebecca's question."

"Chad wasn't lying." Mallory bit one of her nails. "The situation's hard to explain."

Rebecca put her hands on her hips. "Try us."

"You're gonna have to take our word for it," Archie said.

"Nice try," Dan said.

"We're here to have a good time," Archie said.

Oh, Archie. If only he sold his comment with more confidence. At least then the frown lines on Rebecca's face might've disappeared, because if Archie's life depended on Rebecca believing him, then he was two seconds away from dying.

Rebecca clutched her necklace. "Yeah, and I'm the President of the United States."

"Let it go," I said.

"We don't have time for this." Archie put an arm around both Mallory's and my arm before we started walking away, but Rebecca and Dan cut us off from going any farther.

"Why are you being such a bitch?" Mallory asked.

"You did not just call me that," Rebecca said.

Getting dragged into a murder wasn't bad enough. My head ached, and I couldn't wait to go home and take an aspirin. I needed all of five seconds to realize how Mallory and Rebecca might make life more annoying.

Dan let out a breath. "What's wrong with caring what happens to your friends?"

Mallory raised her eyebrows. "What makes you think something is wrong?"

"It's written on your faces," Rebecca said.

"And you would've told us if you planned on attending the dance," Dan said.

I glanced at Mallory and Archie. "We don't have a choice."

"You can't be serious?" Mallory demanded.

Archie touched his eyelid. "Chad's right."

Caring about selfishly dragging Dan and Rebecca into this mess didn't matter. If they knew what happened, then I might have allies. No matter how much I hoped my friendship with Mallory would return to normal, I couldn't ignore how the current drama was Mallory's fault. If she'd just moved on with her life and hadn't blackmailed Tommy, then he wouldn't have later blackmailed her. And as much as I might've wanted to, I might not have been able to trust her anymore. Especially when feelings were on the line.

Mallory hissed. "Fine. We'll tell you what's going on. But not here. Let's find an empty hallway."

SATURDAY, DECEMBER 8, 2018

I walked into the kitchen, only to be greeted by Mom. She sported her bathrobe and stood by the stove while bacon sizzled in the frying pan.

She flashed a smile. "Morning, honey."

"Morning."

"I thought bacon and eggs would be a nice treat."

Normally, there was nothing like bacon's greasy odor wafting through the air to get me excited about starting the day. But not today. Not when I couldn't wish away everything that happened in the last twenty-four hours, because Mallory was right. Sleuthing only got me into trouble, and I should've let Mallory and Archie hang.

"Something wrong?" Mom asked.

"I'm stressed about school."

"It's okay if you're hungover..."

I remained silent.

"Just tell me because I have the best hangover cure known to man," Mom continued.

"I'm fine," I said.

If only the universe weren't so cruel.

Even I appreciated the twisted irony of Mom giving me something without hesitation. The problem was, it wasn't what I needed, because a hangover was preferable to wondering if Tommy was still alive or if I'd be implicated in a murder.

"Are you sure you're okay?" Mom flipped the bacon with a spatula.

"You were in high school once and understand how too much is expected from teens."

"True."

Mom squealed. "I'm glad you attended the dance—you can't worry about school 24/7; it's not healthy."

MONDAY, DECEMBER 10, 2018

Dan, Rebecca, Mallory, Archie, and I stood by my locker while a couple of students and teachers walked through the hallway. Various voices hadn't filled the hallway yet, so I had time to convince myself today would be another normal day of classes I wouldn't care about two days from now.

"The news would've mentioned if a body was found," Rebecca said.

Mallory gave Rebecca a dirty look. "Not so loud."

"Calm down," Dan said.

Rebecca twirled a strand of her hair. "You did the right thing in telling us."

"I wanna know how a body and gun disappear," Archie said.

I snickered. "Maybe we'll never know."

"Either Tommy got up and left, or someone took his body out of the house," Archie said.

Footsteps echoed through the hallway, and we whipped our bodies around.

My focus should've remained on getting my stuff for my morning classes, though. At least then I wouldn't have to deal with the girl getting closer and closer to us. Even if the Aviator sunglasses wrapped around her face ensured not worrying about eye contact.

Rebecca wrinkled her nose. "Are you hungover, Gemma?"

"Just upset," Gemma snapped.

Mallory gritted her teeth. "Why?"

Regardless of how I felt about Mallory, I couldn't deny she had guts. I wouldn't have spoken to Gemma if she were the last person on Earth. Doing so would've been too gutsy in light of everything that happened in the last few days.

Gemma grimaced. "Playing dumb only gets you so far, Mallory."

Mallory's lips quivered. "What do you mean?"

"You're a smart girl, so figure it out," Gemma said.

Rebecca crossed her arms. "If you hate her, then you should give her a reason."

"I was supposed to meet someone after the Snowflake Ball, but the guy never showed." Gemma paused for a second. "And God help whoever ruined my plans."

We all continued staring at Gemma while the vein on her forehead almost popped. Good gracious. Couldn't say I was excited for what she was about to say.

"And that's not the only thing that's happened recently," Gemma said. "My father's gun is missing from his safe."

Yup. The Tommy situation was more complex than Rebecca, Dan, Mallory, Archie, and I realized. If Tommy stole his father's gun, and that reappeared with his body, then the police might get to the truth faster than they hoped. The next question would be why Tommy needed a gun, which could lead back to Mallory blackmailing him to leave town and him blackmailing her for more money.

Archie's Adam's apple throbbed. "Hopefully, your situation improves."

"Doubtful. Some endings are final. Anyway, have a great day. Although something tells me we'll be seeing a lot of each other." Gemma strutted the down the hallway and was soon out of earshot.

None of us spoke, at least not yet. Instead, we exchanged glances. We didn't have to be psychic to know what was on all our minds.

"Was Gemma gonna leave town with Tommy?" Archie asked.

Mallory shrugged. "I don't know, but I wish I did."

Wow. What a shocker. For once, Mallory couldn't invent a snide comment, and I'd have to alert every media outlet in the country.

I scrunched my eyebrows. "You heard her. Gemma did everything but accuse us."

"Tommy must be dead," Mallory murmured.

"Then where the hell is his body and gun?" Archie demanded.

"Doesn't matter. If anyone asks, we had no link to Tommy that night," Mallory said.

We all nodded, yet the empty feeling in my stomach grew. We could push whatever narrative we wanted, but if we didn't know where the body was, then we weren't in control of the situation. And that fact provided more misery than summer school. Wondering when and where a dead body would appear was no way to live.

BEFORE

WEDNESDAY, SEPTEMBER 5, 2018

Time for more deep breaths.

Some clichés such as people only living once were true. So, I had to forget about my pride—or how my heart must've been beating so fast that it should've exploded—and walk over to Archie's locker and talk to him before the first period bell rang. More specifically, maybe ask him out. Nothing formal. Maybe coffee or frozen yogurt. Something that was fun but didn't scream desperate.

I tapped his shoulder. "Hi."

"Hi yourself."

"Do you have a second?" I asked.

"Anything for you."

I coughed, clearing the scratchiness from my throat. No need to panic. What I was about to do was normal. The worst outcome was that Archie wasn't interested and I'd move onto the next person.

Archie reciprocating would've made life simpler, though. And not because I would've damned him to Hell if I didn't get my way. I couldn't stop cringing from yesterday when Mallory was watching me in the school hallway. She didn't have to say or do anything malicious for me to call bullshit. There was just something about the look in her eyes and smirk on her face that made me stare at my bedroom ceiling way longer than I should've last night.

He laughed. "Were you gonna say something?"

"Sorry. I need to stop getting distracted."

"No worries," Archie said.

"I was wondering if you'd want to go out sometime. Perhaps this weekend?"

He drew in a breath. "Wow. I'm flattered…"

Great. Great. Great. I didn't need a PhD to know what would happen next. Mentioning being flattered must've been his way of preparing to let me down. Wow. The universe's cruel irony never stopped. One moment I rejected someone, and the next moment someone rejected me.

"But I can't," Archie said.

I clenched my jaw. "Did I misread the situation? Are you straight?"

"It's not that…"

"Then what?" I demanded.

"Someone already asked me out." Archie grabbed the last textbook from his locker, tossed it into his backpack, then zipped it up.

Damn the universe. If Archie was straight, then the room wouldn't have been spinning. At least then I would've known I did everything I could. But no. The universe had to give its usual fucked up twist to my life. The only thing crueler than someone not reciprocating feelings was being too late to the opportunity.

My mouth gaped. "Oh…"

"I'm sorry, Chad."

No offense to Archie, but he shouldn't have apologized to me. Doing so only made the situation worse. Pity shouldn't have been linked to romantic situations—whether in a small way or in a big way.

I lowered my gaze. "Don't worry about it."

"If only you got to me sooner," Archie said.

"I didn't misread the situation?"

He frowned. "I already answered your question."

No need for a raised voice. I was the one who resembled a child who made a birthday list, only to be denied every item from it. And that was fine. I'd pick myself up eventually.

I looked away. "Sorry."

"I really was flirting with you yesterday," he said.

"Thanks for your honesty," I said.

How kind of him to reassure me the situation wasn't all in my head. Almost as if his words were a magical fix.

"Don't mention it. Nobody deserves to be strung along."

I let out a nervous laugh. "Good to know I'm not a complete idiot and can still navigate social situations."

Archie raised his eyebrows. "Is your self-esteem that low?"

"Yeah," I whispered.

"We can be friends..."

"Sure."

The warning bell for first period screeched, and I shuddered. My conversation with Archie had been going on longer than I realized. However, rage wasn't pulsing through my body from our conversation being cut short. If anything, the universe did me a kindness. For the moment, Archie and I had nothing left to discuss.

He slid his fingers through his hair. "I should get going, but see you in math class later."

"Sounds good."

Tears pricked my eyes while I continued standing in the hallway, and dozens of students scurried by me. Almost as if I were a tourist drifting through New York City. The person I was most pissed off at was myself. Somehow, I allowed myself to become intoxicated by the novelty of getting to know somebody new. And that was no way to live. Crushes and attraction might've been normal, yet I had to live life for myself, not someone else.

I couldn't help wondering one thing, though. The identity of the person who asked Archie out. The situation felt convenient, and I prayed the burning feeling in my throat was from drinking my morning coffee too fast and not something more sinister.

THURSDAY, SEPTEMBER 6, 2018

I exited my car in the high school parking lot while sun beamed from the sky and chirping birds perched on a nearby tree. Just because my current surroundings might've made for the perfect painting didn't mean life was perfect. Mallory just got out of the car parked several spaces from mine and was headed towards me.

She grinned. "Lovely morning, isn't it?"

"What's up?" I asked.

"No need to be curt."

"How am I supposed to react?" I asked.

She gripped one of her pigtails. "I don't want there to be any awkwardness between us."

I must've been in an alternate dimension. The universe couldn't have been gracious enough to let Mallory and I resume our friendship. Life wasn't that simple. Not when the universe could've fucked me over a million different ways.

I blinked. "Really?"

"Our friendship is worth more than my silly crush."

"It's not silly. I just didn't feel the same way."

"I should thank you," she said.

"For what?" I asked.

She remained silent for a second. "For not leading me on. Most guys wouldn't have been so kind."

"Don't sell yourself short. Anyway, should we start walking inside so we can get to our lockers?" I asked.

She nodded. "Sure. I have no problem with walking and talking at the same time."

My pulse lowered while we started walking to the front entrance. Whether I shared my feelings with Mallory or not didn't matter. Having our friendship heal itself was one miracle I'd accept. I deserved something to go right for once in my life. Especially in light of Archie shooting me down yesterday.

Mallory winked. "What's new with you?"

"You don't wanna know," I said.

She came to an abrupt halt. "You can tell me anything—you know that."

"It's embarrassing."

"I promise not to laugh."

Being vulnerable with Mallory didn't mean our friendship would be perfect. However, it was a step in our friendship returning to normal. So, I'd probably tell her about the Archie situation. That was what friends were for, after all. Hell, she might've been able to give me insight that I missed.

Besides, I was still allowed to obsesses about Archie a little while longer—it was barely twenty-four hours since our fateful conversation.

"I asked a guy out," I blurted.

Her eyes lit up while we were now a few feet away from my school's main entrance. "And?"

"It didn't go as I wanted," I said.

"I'm sorry to hear that. Is it possible that you misread the situation? That's happened to me before."

Regardless of how being on speaking terms with Mallory might've been good, I almost shook my head. I would've been obtuse if I didn't consider how her comment might've been a jab at me. Perhaps she misread our friendship and thought I liked her even if she'd never admit said fact to me.

"No, he's bi," I said.

"Then what's the problem?"

"Someone beat me to it," I revealed.

"That's terrible," Mallory said.

Wow. Maybe Mallory and I had more in common than I realized. Labeling a situation worse than it actually was described me to a T.

I shrugged after we turned the corner in the hallway. "It happens."

"I'm flattered you're confiding in me."

"Enough serious talk. Tell me how your first week of school is going," I said.

Mallory didn't speak.

"Did I say something wrong?" I asked.

"I don't want to upset you…" Mallory said.

"I'm fine."

"I asked a guy out and he said yes. I can show you his Facebook page." Mallory grabbed her iPhone from her pocket, then handed it to me. "Isn't he hot? And get this. He moved to town this week. I mean, how lucky am I that the new kid is interested in me?"

What most people didn't understand was that shock didn't always happen in life or death situations. The sensation also occurred in quieter moments. Like when the grocery store was out of my favorite dessert, my favorite restaurant closed, or when my best friend did something more awkward than admitting her crush on me.

She took her iPhone back from me. "Something wrong?"

"I'm glad something is going right for one of us."

Mallory squealed. "I feel the same way. Anyway, don't worry. We'll find you a hot guy in no time. If there's hope for me, then there's hope for you."

Mallory could've told me Mom died and my insides wouldn't have been filled with so much dread. Spying on me when I talked to Archie, plus the identity of the guy she was going out with, couldn't have been a coincidence. My intuition was always right, and I'd have to contemplate if I'd be able to be friends with her—or the very least, be able to trust her. Just because I didn't accuse her of doing something despicable, didn't mean I couldn't beware of her—I deserved to protect myself.

FRIDAY, SEPTEMBER 7, 2018

I was about to walk into the library instead of going to the cafeteria for lunch when I bumped into Rebecca and Dan.

Rebecca grinned. "Hi, Chad. Long time no chat. How has your first week been going?"

"Fine," I said.

Dan tugged at his cardigan sweater. "Don't you think we deserve better than a one word answer?"

Fantastic. As if I didn't have enough to contemplate. Nope. I needed the universe to pile on as much bullshit as possible. Doing so ensured I had a better life.

"Something wrong?" Rebecca asked.

"How's your painting going?" I asked.

"I'm more interested in how you're doing," Rebecca said.

"Is there a reason why you haven't been at lunch the last few days?" Dan asked.

"Doesn't matter," I said.

Rebecca put her hands on her hips. "Let us be the judge of that."

Rebecca might've been putting on her tough girl act, but if I could deal with the last couple of days, then I could tolerate her. Regardless of the numerous contradictory emotions I'd felt, I was still standing, and that counted for something. I might not have been perfect, but I didn't have to be a genius to realize some people might not have been able to handle a possible duplicitous best friend.

"You have no idea what you're talking about," I said.

Dan pouted. "Then tell us. We can help you."

Rebecca let go of Dan's hand. "Just because we're dating, doesn't mean we don't have time for you."

"Did something happen to Tommy? Did Mallory tell you something that the police haven't told anyone?" Dan asked.

Funny he mentioned Mallory. I so wanted to discuss Mallory. It wasn't as if I thought about her enough already.

I took in the longest breath of my life. "Fine. You want to know the truth? I was gonna ask out the new kid, Archie."

"Okay…" Rebecca said.

"But Mallory beat me to it," I interrupted.

Dan chuckled. "Did he send you mixed signals? He's in my English class and could benefit from being knocked down a peg or two."

"This isn't about his signals," I said.

"Then what?" Rebecca demanded.

Yup. It was time to verbalize the thought in my head. The thought I'd been too afraid to utter, because it couldn't be true. The thought that might force me to consider whether I could handle being Mallory's friend.

"Mallory probably asked Archie out to get back at me because I rejected her on the first day of school when she confessed her crush on me," I said before unzipping my backpack and taking a sip from my water bottle.

Dan's eyes bulged. "That's a mouthful."

"No shit," I said.

Rebecca scratched her neck while a couple of students walked by us. "You don't think Mallory is that vindictive, do you?"

"I don't know what to think." I looked Dan in the eye. "And for the record, Archie plays for both teams."

"Good to know," Dan said.

Rebecca pushed her headband further up her head. "I'm sorry about this."

I expelled a mock laugh. "I sound like a deranged fool."

Rebecca grabbed my hand. "You aren't delusional, your feelings are just hurt. And it's understandable. But if you're this upset, then you should do something. At least then, you'll know you tried."

"I can't get into a fight at school," I said.

"Then confront them on their date," Dan said.

I whipped my head back and forth. "I have no idea where they're hanging."

Rebecca giggled. "I do. Mallory told me about meeting a new friend Saturday at noon at Café Tomorrow. However, I didn't realize it was a date."

"You don't think I should crash their date?" I asked.

Dan smirked. "It might give you closure."

I stroked my chin while the whole Mallory and Archie situation lingered on my mind. Perhaps Mallory showed me who she was going out with to rub it in. Especially if she'd seen Archie and I talking on the first day of school. Yet my suspicion couldn't be true. Mallory's deception seemed too convoluted—even for hurt feelings. Schemes were supposed to unfold on soap operas, not in the school hallway.

SATURDAY, SEPTEMBER 8, 2018

Someone should've given me a Nobel Peace Prize.

I was about to accost Archie and Mallory—who happened to be seated at a table outside, in front of Café Tomorrow—and I hadn't even taken a shot of whiskey.

"Fancy seeing you two here," I said.

Mallory lifted her gaze off the table while the café's neon open sign continued glowing. "What are you doing?"

Archie waved at me. "Hi."

I sucked on my teeth. "I know everything, Mallory."

"Excuse me?" she asked.

"I saw you watching me in the hallway on the first day of school, and I'm pretty sure you saw my entire conversation with Archie," I said.

Someone should've pinched me.

The kid who never spoke in class wasn't supposed to defend himself. Yet here I was, fighting for what I wanted. Doing so was the least I deserved. If I spoke up and didn't get the outcome I wanted, then I would've let the situation go. At least then, I would've known I did everything I could.

Mallory rose, then pushed in her chair. "What are you implying?"

"And you just had to show me the photo of the guy you asked out," I said.

"I'm not following," Mallory said.

I shrieked at her. "Cut the bullshit. You're hanging with Archie to get back at me—don't deny it."

"That's absurd," Mallory said.

Archie stood. "Is it possible you're overreacting?"

"I have nothing to gain by interrupting your date and embarrassing myself," I said.

"You've always been desperate," Mallory said.

I locked my arms together. "It's not desperate if it's true."

Archie turned to Mallory. "Is Chad correct? Are you using me because you thought Chad liked me?"

Wow. Maybe life wasn't 100 percent gloom and doom. Archie didn't have to push Mallory for answers, yet he had. Almost as if he entertained the possibility of me being correct. Or at least I hoped he did. I deserved nice things too.

"You're still hot," Mallory said.

I rolled my eyes. "Unbelievable."

Archie's lips curled. "You aren't gonna deny the accusation?"

"There's no point," Mallory said.

A lump lingered in Archie's throat. "I'm so sorry, Chad. If I had known that Mallory was your friend, then I would've never gone out with her."

"Doesn't matter. I won; Chad lost," Mallory said.

Scheming and hurt feelings was one thing, yet Mallory needed to check herself before doing anything else stupid. Life wasn't a game, and Archie and I didn't deserve to be treated like pawns. One day, she could piss off the wrong person. Like someone with a temper.

AFTER

TUESDAY, DECEMBER 11, 2018

"This was so wrong." Archie turned to me while the bed comforter remained wrapped around us as we lay in my bed. Afternoon sunlight poked through my bedroom curtains; there wasn't one cloud in the sky.

I'd have to seriously consider what Archie just said, though. If we wanted to fix things, then we needed to be in agreement about our dynamic.

I snickered. "I disagree."

"You would."

"You admitted you ended things with me because of Mallory, not because you stopped caring about me."

Archie wiped a bead of sweat from his forehead. "True."

"This isn't about hurting Mallory, it's about doing what's right."

"If you say so."

I rolled my eyes. "You don't regret coming over, do you?"

My question had to be asked regardless of how I should've had more confidence in myself. The only guarantee in life was that I couldn't be certain of anything—whether it be my friendship with Mallory, Archie and I having a chance at real romance or if we were all gonna go down for Tommy's murder. My sweat-laced palms felt as natural as breathing, since being in a heightened emotional state was about the only thing I knew how to do.

"No, I wanted to sleep with you," Archie replied.

"I knew you couldn't stay away."

He elbowed me. "Don't be arrogant. Nobody likes a fuckboy."

"Don't call me that."

He tapped my nose. "Take a joke."

"It's hard to have a sense of humor when we might go down for murder." I wet my right index finger, then wiped the dust off the mahogany table next to my bed. If life would always be a roller coaster, then I could at least have a clean room. Or perhaps I wanted something—anything—that distracted me from the possibility of disappointment with Archie. The idea wasn't a stretch. I long ran out of fingers for the number of times the universe took a dump on me over the years—situations sometimes had to be labeled as I saw them.

"Don't be dramatic," Archie said.

"His body has to turn up eventually regardless of what you, Mallory, Dan, and Rebecca are hoping for."

"True. It'd be nice to know where the body is."

Maybe Archie and I had more of a connection than I realized. One agreement didn't mean life would be perfect, yet he must've cared about what I thought if he understood the location of Tommy's body was an important issue to me.

"Do you think anyone knows what we did?" I asked.

"Like Gemma?"

I slouched. "I don't know. I was literally talking about anyone."

Archie exhaled. "Just because I wanted this, doesn't mean it can happen again."

There it was, the universe's delightful sense of humor. It never hesitated to give me the double middle finger. My renewed dynamic with Archie couldn't have been over before it began.

I licked my lips. "You've lost me."

"We shouldn't be sneaking behind Mallory's back. Do you want our love triangle to implode our murder situation?"

"What should we do?" I demanded.

"I don't know." Archie sat up in bed, grabbed his boxers, then slid into them. "But I don't trust myself to keep my hands off you."

Hahaha. I knew I wasn't in denial about our chemistry. People that weren't meant to be together should've had no problem controlling themselves. Although someone should've dumped a bucket of ice on me. I never once anticipated how I'd be the horny teenager I mocked when watching television shows and movies.

I pulled his arm. "Don't be ridiculous!"

"I'm not saying we shouldn't be together…"

Good. Because if he suggested we couldn't be together for reasons others than him not caring about me like that, then we'd have a serious problem. If we wanted to be together, then we needed to just be together. No excuses.

"Answer my question," I said.

"Some problems don't have an easy solution."

I blinked. "I'm a burden?"

"Don't put words in my mouth—you know what I meant."

I ran my fingers through his hair—as if caressing him might change his mind. "Don't go."

"I'm open to suggestions," Archie said.

Easier said than done. I was a big enough person to appreciate how some situations were beyond my comprehension. Like if Mallory got jealous if Archie and I resumed our relationship.

My gaze shifted to his waist, then I resumed eye contact. "I had one idea. But you have to trust me."

"You have my attention."

I scooted downward a few inches before pulling his plaid boxers down to his ankles and wrapping my hands around his waist. So, what if I was gonna go to Hell for using sex to manipulate Archie. It wasn't as if I didn't care about him. We just needed a moment of pleasure—it was the least we deserved after everything we'd been through over the last few days.

WEDNESDAY, DECMBER 12, 2018

Archie and I kept exchanging glances while we sat at a table inside Café Tomorrow, as opposed to outside. The chill in the air was just too much—almost as if my bones ached from thinking about winter.

Just because we knew what we had to do, didn't mean it'd be easy. A good chance existed that our talk with Mallory would go wrong and only complicate the Tommy situation.

Footsteps shuffled against the tiled floor, then Archie and I looked up.

Mallory grunted. "Please provide context next time you want an impromptu hangout. Especially given everything that's happened."

I bit my lip. "Sorry."

Mallory pulled out the chair and sat down at our table. "It's fine. Just don't let it happen again."

"Understood," Archie said.

I pushed the mug towards Mallory. "We ordered for you. We know how you love your caramel macchiatos like me."

"Thanks." Mallory grabbed the mug. Except she didn't sip her beverage. Instead, she pressed the cup against her cheeks while steam seeped from the top. She resembled Mom—using a cup to provide extra warmth was something Mom would've done.

Archie coughed. "We wanted to be honest with you."

Shit. We were really gonna do this, and there was no turning back, so I'd have to cross my fingers if I wanted this conversation to remain civil.

"What are you talking about?" Mallory asked.

Archie squeezed my hand. "Chad and I want to get back together."

"What about everything that happened?" Mallory demanded.

"You were using Archie because you were scared," I said.

Archie gave me a look, then resumed eye contact with Mallory. "I'm not mad at you; I just want to get on with my life."

"Okay," Mallory said.

I furrowed my eyebrows. "You aren't pissed?"

"How much of a bitch do you think I am?" Mallory asked.

"At least we're being honest with each other," Archie said.

Mallory smiled. "Exactly. If we've learned one thing, it's that secrets cause the most harm, not the actual deed."

Shutting up and being thankful was sometimes the best someone could do. The old me might've chastised the universe for giving me something unexpected—even if it was something that I wanted—but not now. Too much had happened. I also owed it to myself to pursue my own happiness. And if that meant dating Archie, then great. It wasn't like I lost all sense of independence because of having a boyfriend—I was just human and couldn't be alone.

Mallory exhaled. "I'm not lost to how this couldn't have been easy for you."

"You have no idea," I said.

Just because I wouldn't criticize her for making me sweat for nothing, didn't mean I turned my brain off. I owed myself honesty. Like wondering if Mallory was having a delayed reaction to my news. Even if I should've been content with the sugar high from the copious amount of whipped cream the barista put on my latte.

Mallory sipped her caramel macchiato. "Let's make each other a promise. No more secrets."

Archie and I looked at each other, then nodded at Mallory.

"Good. I think we'll be fine," Mallory said.

THURSDAY, DECEMBER 13, 2018

I didn't have to be a runway model to strut the school hallway before first period.

Just like I deserved to see if resuming my relationship with Archie would make me happy, I also deserved for my heart not to thump a thousand miles a minute. Mallory was okay with Archie, and for now I'd take at her feelings at face value. Doing otherwise would've only complicated my life, and I couldn't have that.

Except I didn't count on running into Mallory's sister, even if she was my high school's new creative writing teacher. She just started teaching this school year, which was kind of impressive. Most people might not have gotten a job right out of grad school.

She tugged at my wrist. "Do you have a second, Chad?"

I pushed her hand off me. "What's up?"

Kelly flashed a gold watch at me. "I think you left this at my house."

"Thanks," I said, taking my watch back. Yet I didn't put it on my right wrist yet. Not when I couldn't fathom how I'd be reckless enough to misplace my watch the night of Tommy's "murder." Especially since it was the last gift Dad got me before he got cancer and subsequently died.

"No problem."

I took in a breath. "I'm impressed with you."

Kelly a blew a chunk of her auburn hair out of the way. "And why is that?"

"Most people wouldn't be enthusiastic about taking care of their sibling," I said.

"It's not like I have a choice—our parents are dead."

"I know, I know," I said. "But it's a little more than a year since they died."

She gripped her silver bracelet. "Do you mind if I ask a question?"

"Go ahead."

"Has Mallory seemed different to you?" Kelly asked.

Way to ask a loaded question. Yeah. Mallory was different. She caused Tommy's death, and now Dan, Rebecca, Archie, and I had to live with what happened. Almost as if we got our own version of a death sentence.

"What do you mean?" I fanned myself with my shirt. Just because winter was inching closer and closer didn't mean I couldn't feel like I was in the Sahara Desert. The school must've cranked up the heat too high. Either that, or I was having a panic attack and I'd soon have the all-too-familiar dizzy sensation.

"She's been in a funk ever since the day after the Snowflake Ball."

No shit. I'd be a wreck if I killed someone. But I was at school, so I had to keep the venom to a minimum. One wrong move, and the situation would implode.

"I'm sure it's school stress," I said.

She bobbed her head. "That's what I thought. Also, don't tell Mallory about my question. No need to upset her."

"I know how to keep a secret."

Kelly winked. "I'm sure you can. Although I also have discretion, so don't hesitate to confide in me if you ever find yourself in a predicament. Anyway, have a good day."

She walked away, leaving me to myself.

Just because I couldn't predict the future, didn't mean I couldn't delude myself into thinking life would be okay. Everyone deserved occasional indulgences like denial. Especially when Tommy's body was still out there somewhere, waiting to be discovered.

BEFORE

MONDAY, SEPTMBER 17, 2018

He waved at me. "Hi, Chad."

Crap. Running into Archie in the school hallway on my way to lunch was the last thing that should've happened. 48 hours hadn't even passed since I confronted Mallory on her coffee date with Chad.

I couldn't scurry away from Archie, though. Not when he was fast approaching. If I didn't talk to him now, then he might find me later. So, I'd suck it up and get the conversation over with—even if there were 1,001 other things I would've rather been doing. Like swimming with sharks, attending summer school, or meeting a venomous snake.

Archie sighed. "I'm sorry about everything."

The universe might've been a lot of things, yet I never expected Archie to apologize. He hadn't betrayed me.

"It's fine," I said.

"I would've never gone out with Mallory if I knew the whole situation."

"What's done is done."

"Don't be like this. You're clearly upset."

"I'm young; I'll get over it."

He bit his lip. "You don't have to put on a façade for me."

"What? Am I supposed to be thrilled that I'm your second choice?"

Interrupting Archie and Mallory's date was one thing, yet I would've rather died than be with someone who treated me as an afterthought.

Relationships couldn't be forced and had to happen on their own. If they didn't, then they were doomed before they started.

Archie coughed. "I would've said yes if you asked me the first day of school."

"There's no way of knowing that."

"I wouldn't lie—not about something so serious," Archie said.

Yeah, right. A difference existed between saying something and actually doing it. I also didn't know Archie well enough to figure out if he were telling the truth. And for all I knew, Archie might've used that line on other people.

"What do you want?" I asked.

"Let's try this again."

I narrowed my gaze. "What about Mallory?"

"Do you seriously think I'm still interested in her after what happened?"

Good question. The cynic in me would've been skeptical of Archie's comment. Something about disturbed people being the wildest in bed—at least according to pop culture.

"It's too late," I said.

"What she did was fucked up."

Deep breaths. If I didn't watch what I said, then I'd seem unhinged. And I couldn't have that. Not putting my fists through a wall because of Mallory's behavior took all the energy I had and more and more students were walking through the hallway.

"No need to state the obvious," I said.

"Don't be curt; I'm trying to empathize with you."

"You don't owe me anything."

He folded his arms. "Why are you doing this? We can hang."

Archie might've been a lot of things, but I couldn't say he gave up easily. Most people might not have had the patience to deal with me.

"Were you really flirting with me on the first day of school?" I asked.

"Yes. I might not know a lot about you, but you seem like an interesting person. Not every guy is platinum blond."

Interesting person. Please. He'd have to try harder if he wanted my attention. Anyone could've called me an interesting person. If he wanted to impress, then he'd have to say something only he'd say. I also couldn't help wondering if my stance turned him on—some people loved a challenge. Although I'd cringe if that were true. Archie shouldn't have wanted something just because he couldn't have it.

"Thanks," I forced.

"Come on. What do you say? We can go to Starbucks after school."

"No thanks."

Nope. I wouldn't budge no matter how ridiculous Archie might've thought my behavior was. Protecting myself was my biggest priority. I didn't owe Archie anything. And soon, this whole situation could be forgotten about.

"What? You're gonna let your pride stop you from getting what you want?"

I grunted. "How'd you act if you were me?"

"I'd stop being friends with Mallory, that's for sure."

"Take care of yourself." I almost walked away from Archie when he grabbed my arm. Then, every neuron in my body became electrified while blood pumped through my body faster and I almost choked. Even the smallest gesture showed intimacy, because Archie and I couldn't have been closer if I tried.

He grimaced. "Mallory told me about your dad right after you left."

Archie had to be careful about the next words that came out of his mouth. Mentioning Dad wasn't something that should've been done lightly. Archie also shouldn't have talked about things he had no firsthand knowledge about—like a medical student expecting to perform surgery on the first day of medical school.

"What does he have to do with anything?" I asked.

"Pushing people away is your defense mechanism," Archie said.

I shoved Archie's arm off me. "I'm sure Mallory couldn't wait to tell you about my dad."

"She wasn't trying to hurt you—at least not this time."

"Sure," I said.

A lump lingered in Archie's throat. "I'm sure you're probably tired of dealing with disappointment."

No offense to Archie, but he needed to be more mindful of where the conversation was going. It wasn't his job or right to psychoanalyze. Until Archie understood what my life was like, he needed to keep quiet.

"Tell me something I don't know," I said.

"I'm giving you what you want."

The bell rang and I cursed under my breath. Just because nobody took attendance during lunch, didn't mean I had to arrive late. If anything, getting to the lunch line early was best. Having to wait in a long line was one of the most eye-roll-inducing events in the world.

"You don't have to give me anything," I said.

Archie stomped his feet against the tile floor. "What more do I have to say?"

"There's nothing you can do."

"Your dad would want you to be happy." Archie paused for a beat. "And there's no reason why we can't still have fun."

I fought back the tears while standing in silence. My grief would always exist no matter how much I suppressed my feelings, and that loss felt like an uninvited guest crashing a party.

"Don't mention my father!" I exclaimed. "You didn't see him being taken away in a body bag."

Archie clapped his hand over his mouth. "I'm sorry; I had no idea."

WEDNESDAY, SEPTMBER 19, 2018

I shuffled through the high school parking lot after parking my car while gray-tinged clouds remained stacked in the sky.

Great. As if I needed another reminder that life was shitty. I so wanted to be the idiot who forgot his umbrella.

The impending rain wasn't my biggest problem, though. Mallory just walked up to me, which sucked. Talking to Mallory wasn't what I needed for my day to be perfect. If I wasn't careful, then she'd hurt me.

"You haven't returned my texts," she said.

Mallory must've been more delusional than I realized. I wouldn't have corresponded with her if my life depended on it. I had too much self-respect to associate with someone who was as heartless as she was. If roles were reversed, then she might've been furious with me if I'd pulled the same crap she had.

I snorted. "Take a hint."

"Are you really gonna cut me out of your life?"

Sorry, not sorry. I wouldn't waste any tears on Mallory. She made the decision to pursue Archie to hurt me. And now she'd have to live with her choice. This wasn't some Disney movie where a conflict resolved itself in favor of a miraculous happy ending.

"You don't have much ground to stand on, Mallory," I said. "You're the one who boasted about your win."

She looked at the ground. "Fine. That was too much."

"How could you do this to me?" I demanded.

"It's just one guy."

"It's not the point."

"I did what I had to do. You rejected me, only to start chatting with another guy moments later."

Infatuation was one thing, yet Mallory needed a serious dose of reality ASAP. There should've been more to her life than whether or not I rejected her. I wasn't the only guy out there, and she could find a boyfriend—that wasn't Archie or me—if she really wanted to.

"It's done, Mallory," I spat.

"Don't be like this. You can have Archie if you want."

"He's not a toy."

"I never said he was."

The trees bobbed in the wind and rain pattered against the ground.

Fantastic. It wasn't like I hoped the rain would wait till I got inside. Nope. I dreamed of being rained on. My life was dull and needed more excitement. Maybe there'd even be a tornado, and I'd get swept away to Oz.

"You're just pissed you got caught," I said.

"Fine. That might be true. But I miss being friends with you, and I'm sure we can work through this."

"I always knew *Cruel Intentions* was your favorite movie, but I never thought you were a sick fuck," I said.

"I made a mistake."

"I don't want to hear from you or know you, so please don't contact me again."

She played with a strand of her hair. "You don't mean that."

"I do."

"You have no idea what my life has been like since summer."

Please. Mallory could reveal the most tragic bombshell, and I wouldn't wince. I didn't owe her anything, and what I thought during my conversation with Archie remained true. I had to look after myself—not anyone else.

I raised my eyebrows. "Are you really gonna play the Tommy card?"

"There's a lot you don't know."

I sneered. "I don't care—I know everything I need to."

"You're gonna regret this."

Mallory should've saved her breath. I would've bet my soul I wouldn't have any regret about cutting her out of my life. If she wanted forgiveness, then she should've tried harder. Friendships weren't like winging a test, they deserved real effort. And so far, Mallory appeared more upset about me rejecting her than our friendship ending.

FRIDAY, SEPTMBER 21, 2018

Flames flickered from the candles on the middle of the dining room table while the greasy scent of pizza wafted through the air. But pizza day didn't mean life was perfect—it wasn't. There was no understanding how I couldn't have realized Mallory was a terrible person years ago.

Mom glanced at my plate, then made eye contact. "You should have your pizza before it gets cold."

"I know, I know."

"You can talk about whatever is upsetting you, because I promise not to judge."

"Thanks."

"I'm serious, Chad." Mom grabbed her glass and sipped her champagne. "I'd want to know if something were wrong."

Mom still needed to watch what she said no matter how well her intentions were. Talking about problems didn't always make life better. If anything, harping on issues made life worse. A person could only talk about a topic for so long—especially a topic like Mallory.

"It's complicated." I grabbed my knife and fork and cut my slice of pizza into bite-size pieces. Yup. I had to be the guy who didn't use his hands for eating pizza. It didn't matter how great the pizza was. Nothing was appealing about getting grease on your hands.

"You can't keep your feelings bottled up."

"Mallory wasn't the person I thought she was," I said.

"I'm sorry to hear that, but do you think you'll be able to mend your friendship?" Mom asked.

I shook my head in a vigorous fashion. "Nope."

"That's too bad. Anyway, you should at least try some champagne."

"I don't know what made you want champagne."

"It's the perfect combination with pizza."

I grabbed my flute, then took a more than generous swig of champagne. Hell, I even smiled for Mom. Regardless of how complicated life was, I couldn't deny she didn't have good taste in alcohol. The champagne contained the perfect mixture of sweet, tart, and carbonated flavors.

"There's something else," I said.

She blinked. "Yes?"

"I pushed someone away just because I had hurt feelings, and now it might be too late."

Yeah. Not wanting to be someone's second choice didn't mean I hadn't been stubborn—I had. Archie was right. I could've gotten what I wanted since he had been more than willing to go out with me. The only problem was I was too concerned about the intoxicated sensation of being in control and saying no. Almost as if hurting Archie—even a small way—allowed me to feel better from the wounds Mallory had inflicted.

"Are you talking about Mallory?" Mom asked.

"No. I'm talking about a guy."

Mom grinned. "Tell me everything."

SATURDAY, SEPTMBER 22, 2018

Rebecca, Dan, and I walked down Main Street while sunlight radiated from the sky and a pigeon landed on the sidewalk.

Having a break from several days of rain wasn't why I halted, though. Archie happened to be standing in front of a coffee shop at the end of block. I hadn't spoken to Archie since our conversation several days ago, and I couldn't help wondering if I should see if his offer still stood.

Rebecca looked at me. "Do you want to talk to him?"

I exhaled. "I don't know."

"You have nothing to lose," Dan said.

"Except my pride," I said.

Rebecca's scarf bobbed in the wind. "Check that. It might be too late."

"What do you mean?" I asked.

"See for yourself," Dan said.

My gaze shifted from Rebecca and Dan and back to Archie at the end of the block. Except Archie was no longer alone. My heart fluttered, but not like opening presents on Christmas morning. Archie was currently involved in a lip lock with my favorite person in the world.

Dan patted my shoulder. "I'm sorry, buddy."

"Don't be. I should've known Mallory would make another play for Archie," I said through gritted teeth.

AFTER

TUESDAY, DECEMBER 18, 2018

Mallory, Dan, Rebecca, Archie, and I were seated at a booth at Deb's Diner on Main Street. Today was a half day because of parent teacher conferences, so we decided to do something spontaneous.

Mallory continued studying the menu. "So many choices."

Dan laughed. "Agreed. It's like going to the Cheesecake Factory."

I closed my menu, then sipped my diet soda. "I'll probably get a burger and fries."

"That doesn't sound exciting," Archie said.

No offense to Archie, but he didn't have to act like my grandmother. Not every conversation had to be a matter of life and death. Or maybe I was making too big a deal out of his comment. He might've just wanted the best for me. And if that were true, then I'd have a real reason for smiling. It wasn't that long ago when Archie and I seemed like we'd never get together, and I'd be destined to watch the Archie and Mallory show. I didn't know what I would've done if that happened.

"I'm fine with that," I said.

Archie winked at me. "Hopefully, we'll have a better meal tomorrow when I meet your mother."

"You're meeting his mom?" Mallory asked.

No need for Mallory to complicate the conversation. This was supposed to be a casual lunch, not chemistry class. Unless Mallory wasn't happy that Archie and I were together. I mean, I had to consider that possibility. People often did one thing while thinking another.

Mallory was also the girl who asked Archie out just to get back at me, and I couldn't forget that fact. Even if our current predicament meant forcing myself to be on good terms with Mallory. People didn't change overnight, so Mallory would always have part of that personality inside her. Even if she might've been doing her best do be a good person.

I snickered. "Yeah. What's the problem?"

Mallory's hair fell behind her shoulders with one swift tilt of her head. "I was just surprised."

"Life goes on, Mallory," I said.

"I thought we were getting along?" Archie asked.

Just because Archie didn't mean harm, didn't mean I liked what he said. Being with me meant not having it both ways. So, if he knew what was best, then he'd take my side the next time Mallory pissed me off.

"She started it," I said.

Rebecca flipped to the menu's next page. "Maybe this wasn't a good idea."

"Don't be ridiculous. Everything is fine," Mallory said.

The waitress arrived at our table a couple of minutes later. "Can I take your orders?"

We all looked at each other, nodding. Then, the waitress left just quickly as she arrived.

It only took me several seconds to start drumming my fingers against the table, though. And the burning, tightened sensation in my throat wasn't because of my grumbling. Nope. I wished this was just a dream after spotting the current headline on the television at the front of the diner. Apparently, earlier today the police found a body in Woodland Park, which was a couple of blocks away from Deb's Diner.

"What's wrong?" Archie asked.

I pointed to the television. "Look!"

Mallory, Rebecca, Dan, and Archie shifted their attention to the television. After that, we all exchanged looks, yet none of us spoke. We had to at least speculate whether the body was Tommy.

Mallory banged her fist against the table. "Fuck!"

"Not so loud," Rebecca said. "Just be glad they didn't mention finding a gun."

Mallory grunted. "I'm sorry. How was I supposed to react?"

"Here you go," said the waitress before placing our plates in front of each of us. "Anyway, let me know if you guys need anything."

"Let's remain calm," Archie said after Beatrice once again left as fast as she arrived.

Dan hissed at us. "If the body turns out to be Tommy, then I want to know who took him out of your house, Mallory."

Goosebumps broke out over my skin, but I couldn't fault Dan for his question. The only way to survive the situation was to be in control of it, and that couldn't happen when we still didn't know a lot.

"Wouldn't we all like to know the answer to that question," I said.

"I'm not one to defend my sister." Mallory grabbed her fork, stabbed her salad, and took a bite of it. "But it couldn't have been my sister who took Tommy's body and gun out of my house."

Mallory's statement should've calmed us, yet my heart pounded faster. If we knew Kelly moved the body and gun, then we would've had an answer. But no. We were just five teenagers winging our way through a situation that we shouldn't have been in. Nothing I ever did was bad enough to justify the dark circles under my eyes since the night of the Snowflake Ball.

"Yeah, yeah. We know she was at the Snowflake Ball," Rebecca said.

I glanced at Mallory. "I've said it before, but I'll say it again: Do you think Gemma was following Tommy that night?"

"I don't know what to think at this point," Mallory said.

Rebecca leaned in. "We need to come up with a plan fast, otherwise we'll get a one-way ticket to jail."

"If you got any ideas, I'm listening," Mallory said.

Funny she should say that. Avoiding responsibility was classic Mallory—whether she accepted the truth or not, she was responsible for our current predicament.

WEDNESDAY, DECEMBER 19, 2018

"This looks great." Archie scooped rice onto his plate, then grabbed a few pieces of the General Tsao's chicken.

Mom giggled. "I just ordered takeout."

"It was a smart move—it takes the pressure off coking," Archie said.

Mom drank the rest of her water. "Exactly."

More moments like this dinner with Archie and Mom should've encompassed my life. Something great existed from Archie agreeing with Mom—even if it wouldn't change how the police found a body. Not every second of the day should've been a struggle.

Mom poured more water from the pitcher on the middle of the dining room table. "Tell me about yourself, Archie."

"I play tennis—although not till the spring."

I chuckled. "I didn't know that."

Yeah. Even I was capable of restraint. No reason existed to be filled with rage. I didn't need to know everything about Archie to be secure in our relationship. A little mystery was also a wonderful thing. Life would've been boring if I knew every detail about him. It wasn't like I thought he'd go back to Mallory just because I was unaware he played lacrosse.

Archie winked. "There's a lot of things you don't know about me."

Mom ate a spoonful of rice. "Get a room."

My cheeks flushed. My sex life—or anything remotely related to that topic—was the last thing I wanted to discuss with my mother. Just like I didn't need to know everything about Archie, Mom didn't need to know everything about me—the world would survive.

Mom grabbed a napkin, then wiped her lip. "Tell me something, Archie. Has Chad ever showed you one of his short stories?"

"No," Archie said.

"Not everything is meant to be shared." I took another bite of my General Tsao's chicken. Yum. Nothing like the mixture of sweet, spicy, and tangy flavors electrifying my taste buds. The dish couldn't have been more perfect if the best chef in the world had prepared the meal.

Mom frowned. "Sharing your writing with your boyfriend is the least you can do. Nobody likes secrets."

Boyfriend. I couldn't deny how it was an interesting word. Regardless of what Archie meant to me, we never once used that word in relation to each other. Yet it was the perfect word to describe Archie, because that was exactly what he was. Even if sometimes, while staring at my bedroom ceiling late at night when I should've been asleep, I wondered if Mallory would ever come between us again.

Archie squeezed my hand. "I'm not gonna force Chad to do anything he doesn't want to."

"That's a great attitude," Mom said. "Anyway, any plans for Christmas vacation, Archie?"

Archie sighed. "No. But I was gonna invite Chad over for Christmas Eve dinner with my family."

I sipped my diet ginger ale.

"What? No reaction to me forgetting to ask you?" Archie continued.

"It's gonna take more than ditsy behavior to scare me away," I said.

Archie should've had more faith in me. Just because I had strong opinions, didn't mean I had to start trouble over every little thing. Contrary to popular opinion, I actually wanted to be happy.

Mom's grin widened. "It's fine with me if Chad wants to spend Christmas Eve with your family, it's not like we do anything."

"Are you sure, Mom?" I asked.

Giving Mom an opportunity to change her mind wasn't about being quirky or neurotic. It was about being a good son. Just because we weren't religious, didn't mean I was oblivious to how it'd be difficult to be alone on a holiday. It was only a couple of years ago that Mom, Dad, and I had our last Christmas together.

I couldn't swallow the lump in my throat. Damn. I couldn't believe that Dad's death wasn't the worst thing I had to suffer through, because I never once considered that I might be arrested someday. Being an accessory to murder wasn't the type of thing most teenagers dreamed about writing for their college essays.

"Yeah, it's fine," Mom said.

Archie looked me right in the eye. In fact, I would've melted if he stared at me with any more intensity. "What do you say?"

I nodded. "I'm in."

"Good. It'll be so great for you to meet my parents and sister," Archie said.

"You have a sister?" I asked.

"Yeah, but I try not to think of her much—she's a real bitch," Archie said. "Although it helps that she's away at college most of the year."

More deep breaths. Not realizing Archie had a sister still wasn't cause for panic. The continued mystery made our relationship more interesting. Besides, I'd take a sibling reveal over the current Tommy drama any day.

THURSDAY, DECEMBER 20, 2018

Leaves crunched underneath my feet while snow fell from the sky. Archie also happened to be walking through the woods with me. Apparently, Mother Nature couldn't wait for winter's official start date for the first snow of the season.

"What was with the cryptic text?" I asked after Archie and I led the group to the clearing in the woods.

"Why does everything have to be an argument with you?" Mallory snapped.

Mallory should've realized the irony of what she said. Every dynamic—whether platonic or romantic—took two people to make work. So, if Mallory expected me to be nice to her, then she also had to pay the same kindness.

Rebecca adjusted her scarf. "Don't start now."

"It's almost Christmas. Let's be nice to each other," Dan said.

Mallory put her hands on her hips. "Don't you watch the news?"

"Yes, but Archie and I have been hanging out all afternoon," I said.

Dan smirked. "Is that a euphemism for something?"

Leave it to Dan to lighten the mood—even if his comment made me nearly as uncomfortable as discussing sex with Mom. I felt exposed, like I was running around naked with all my clothes on.

I shrieked at Dan. "That's none of your business!"

"It's not polite to kiss and tell," Archie said.

Mallory snorted. "I'm gonna be sick."

Mallory shouldn't have responded so cruelly. If she had a problem with Archie and I dating, then she should've said so. Or at least put on a better façade. Even Pinocchio's growing nose would've been more convincing than her current demeanor. If she got one more frown line, the she'd have to get Botox ASAP.

"You said you had something to share?" I asked.

"The police identified the body in Woodland Park," Mallory said.

"And?" I asked.

"It's Tommy," Mallory blurted.

No. No. No. Mallory couldn't have said what she just did. A little unfairness was one thing, yet the universe couldn't have been so mean. Dan, Rebecca, Archie and I didn't deserve to have our lives ruined because of Mallory's drama.

Rebecca put her hands in her jacket pockets. "And you're telling me now?"

"I was waiting for Dumb and Dumber to get here," Mallory said.

Wow. Good to know Mallory had a high opinion of me. It wasn't as if I was helping her avoid arrest or anything.

"Don't talk to us like that," Archie said.

Way to go Archie. About time he picked his balls up off the floor. Some issues were worth fighting for because Archie and I deserved to be treated with respect. Especially if Mallory wanted us to continue helping her.

The wind howled, and clumps of snow fell off the trees. My teeth chattered and I shivered, the temperature so cold that I could see my own breath. So, maybe, just maybe, I shouldn't have worn my basketball shorts tonight.

"Why couldn't we have talked in your bedroom?" I asked.

"Duh! I couldn't risk Kelly overhearing our conversation," Mallory said.

"What do we do?" Archie asked.

"This should be a group vote, but I think we should still stick to the Snowflake Ball—that's our alibi," Mallory said.

I huffed. "Fine. But that still leaves one thing. Who moved the body, and is that person sending the police anonymous tips?"

"That's two things," Mallory said.

"Same difference," I said.

FRIDAY, DECEMBER 21, 2018

Getting excused from a class was the last thing I expected to happen on the Friday before Christmas vacation. That was the type of thing students dreamed about, not something that actually happened.

At my high school, teachers had their own offices so they could meet with students during their free periods, as opposed to one faculty room for the whole department. I opened Kelly's office door and I shook my head. Archie and Mallory were standing in front of Kelly's wooden desk while Kelly remained seated in the swivel chair behind it.

"Shut the door," Kelly said.

I did what she asked. Sometimes, obeying adults was the right thing to do. The contempt radiating from Kelly's eyes couldn't have been faked.

"Why are they here?" I asked.

Kelly slid her elbows onto the table. "They're a part of this like you."

I shrugged. "I don't understand."

"She knows Mallory killed Tommy and that we're covering it up," Archie stammered

Great. Just what my life needed. Another variable. Life was already hard enough as it was, and I deserved a break.

I blinked. "Really?"

Kelly's mouth gaped. "Yup, because I'm the one who disposed of Tommy in Woodland Park, and we're gonna have to come up with a plan if we want to avoid jail."

"Then call Dan and Rebecca to your office, because they're also a part of this," I said.

"Fine, I'll do that," Kelly said. "Do any of you know what class Dan and Rebecca are in right now?"

"Calculus with Mrs. Parks," Mallory said.

"Thanks." Kelly reached for the phone next to her computer, then punched numbers.

"What's going on?" Rebecca asked several minutes later, locking the door once she and Dan stepped into the office.

"We need to get our stories straight," Kelly said.

Rebecca gave Kelly a look. "I don't know what you're talking about."

"She knows about Tommy," Mallory blurted.

Dan laughed. "There's nothing to know."

"Save it," Kelly said. "If the police ask, then you never saw Tommy that night. You guys were at the Snowflake Ball and that's all you need to know."

"We already established this," Rebecca said.

Rebecca should've known better than to make the comment she just had. Any reprieve from class should've been welcomed. Even a discussion about avoiding going to prison because of the Tommy situation. It's not like an opportunity for being an accessory to murder would present itself again. The chance was one of those once in a lifetime things.

Kelly straightened a stack of papers on her desk. "Never hurts to go over the story—the police might talk to you. Tommy and Mallory's relationship was common knowledge, after all."

"I still don't understand why you're involved," Rebecca said.

"She dumped the body in the park," I revealed.

"What about the gun and flash drive?" Dan asked.

"I have them in my bedroom safe," Kelly said.

"Why insert yourself into this?" Rebecca asked.

Mallory sighed. "I was a mess this morning and I had no choice but to reveal the truth. However, I only mentioned Chad and Archie. Chad is the one who mentioned you two."

One. Two. Three. Four. Five.

No big deal about Mallory blaming me. There were more important things worth discussing—like making sure none of us cracked under the pressure. Only one wrong move was required for the situation to implode.

"How did you get rid of the body if you were at the dance?" Rebecca asked.

"I left early because of a migraine," Kelly said.

Rebecca lowered her jaw. "Okay. But what about the bookend?"

"I washed off the blood from it," Kelly said. "Anyway, about that. I'm more concerned about us sticking to your Snowflake Ball alibi no matter what."

"Wait. Have you seen what's on the flash drive?" Dan asked.

"Yes, I know about Gemma and Tommy." Kelly threw a gaze at Mallory, then coughed. "But I'm serious. You guys have your entire lives ahead of you, and don't need to be boggled down by one mistake."

"What are you gonna do if the police get a warrant to search your house?" Rebecca asked. "As you just stated, Tommy and Mallory were dating."

"Let's hope it doesn't come to that," Kelly said.

"What if someone saw you in the woods at the park that night?" Rebecca asked.

"Nobody was around. Anyway, enough questions, so get back to class," Kelly said.

BEFORE

TUESDAY, SEPTEMBER 25, 2018

The knot in my stomach grew while I sat at my desk in baking class.

Everyone else but me somehow partnered up. Well, almost everyone. A girl with jet-black hair extending a few inches below her shoulders remained in her seat, several desks away from me.

She cocked her head. "Partners?"

"Sure, Gemma." I rose, then followed her into the kitchen, which extended from the classroom.

Yup. No reason to be stubborn. If the universe gave me an easy solution, then I'd take it. Nothing bad would happen from working with Gemma—even if she was Tommy's sister. Tommy's "abandonment" and disappearance was another thing I had to live with.

Gemma grinned a couple of minutes later while all the ingredients remained on the kitchen counter. "Wanna do the eggs?"

"Sure," I said, nodding.

"Great. I'll measure the flour, sugar, and oatmeal."

"Sounds like a plan." I grabbed an egg from the carton to the right of me. Then, I cracked it against the metal mixing bowl before repeating the action.

Perfect. Not so much as one bit of eggshell littered the bowl.

She played with a strand of her hair. "You've gotta stir the eggs, genius."

"Sorry."

"Relax. I was teasing."

I grabbed a whisk and stirred the eggs. After that, Gemma mixed the flour, sugar, and oatmeal with the eggs while I lined the tray with aluminum foil. Having the oatmeal cookies stick to the tray was the last thing we needed. There was nothing like cookies that broke when lifting them off the tray.

"And now we wait," Gemma said a couple of minutes later.

"We should be careful not to overcook the cookies. Most recipes overdo it with the suggested bake time."

"I know. This isn't my first-time cooking."

My mouth opened, yet words escaped me. There was no right response to Gemma, because a part of me wondered if she wasn't joking about subtly giving me a hard time. I couldn't imagine what her life might've been like since July. The not knowing if Tommy was alive or dead must've been the worst part. If he was dead, then she'd have an answer. But no. The universe had other plans, as if Gemma was another doll for it to play with.

She giggled. "You don't have to treat me like I'm fragile."

"Come again?"

"I'm coping in light of Tommy."

"I wasn't thinking about Tommy," I said.

Gemma gave me a look. "Yeah, you were, and it's okay. I haven't forgotten your history with him."

"I don't wanna discuss Tommy."

She bit her lip. "Deserting you was cruel."

I forced a laugh. "Shouldn't you take his side?"

"Being related to him doesn't mean liking everything that a person does. It's no secret I wasn't crazy about his relationship with Mallory."

There it was again. The universe forcing me to think about Mallory. It wasn't as if I didn't already replay the image of Mallory and Archie kissing in town the other day dozens of times in my mind like a masochist.

I quirked my eyebrows. "Why would you be jealous of Mallory? You're one of the most popular girls in school."

"Popularity isn't everything, and I still wanna kill Tommy for ditching you for the cool kids—in addition to that other thing he did."

"What? Did you wish you had a boyfriend?" I asked.

Gemma clutched her moon-shaped pendant attached to the necklace looped around her neck. "Something like that."

"There's something that I wanted to ask about Tommy."

"Go for it."

"Wait. Chatting about Tommy isn't too difficult for you?" I demanded.

"It's nice—I'd hate to forget about him. Anyway, you were saying?"

"He didn't cut me off because I came out, did he?"

The warm sugary scent from the oven wafted through the air, and my stomach grumbled. I felt as excited for those cookies as a little kid on Christmas morning waiting to open presents.

"No." Gemma released the pendant from her palm, and it smacked against her chest. "He was just superficial. We have a gay cousin, and he was supportive of him."

A guy from across the room glared at me. In fact, the look surpassed any scowl Mom gave me when I disappointed her. So, yeah. The tightness in my stomach returned. Just because Archie was in my baking class didn't mean I enjoyed said fact. Especially since punching a pillow appealed to me. I wouldn't have let my pride get the better of me in a perfect world and would've just been with Archie regardless of how Mallory chased him first.

"What was that about?" she asked.

"It's complicated."

Gemma snorted. "Let me guess, it's about Archie and Mallory."

"How'd you know?" I asked.

"I've seen them around school a couple of times." Gemma sucked in a breath. "You've gotta be very careful—Mallory can't be trusted. She's poison, and Tommy shouldn't have isolated himself to please her. That's the least of my concerns, though."

I cracked my knuckles. "What do you mean?"

"I wouldn't be surprised if Mallory had something to do with whatever happened to Tommy," Gemma said. "Disappearing within a couple days after they spent the Fourth of July together sounds fishy."

"You must be mistaken." My pulse drummed in my ears. No matter how low my opinion of Mallory was, I wouldn't accuse her of murder. She couldn't have the constitution for killing in light of how worked up she became over our drama.

"I'm not. If there's one thing I learned, it's that anything is possible," Gemma said.

The oven chimed.

Gemma turned the oven off, and she shoved her hands into the mitts. Then, she took the cookies out.

Her warning kept ringing in my mind. Gemma hadn't danced around an accusation, she actually made it.

So, yeah. Gemma might not have been completely wrong. Mallory pursued Archie just to hurt me, so there was no telling what she might've been capable of. However, I still circled back to my previous point. There was a big difference between scheming and killing. Even if the maniacal look in her eyes when she eavesdropped on my first conversation with Archie remained etched in my mind.

WEDNESDAY, SEPTMBER 26, 2018

Before first period, someone tapped my back after I finished taking a drink from the water fountain.

I whipped my body around. "What do you want, Archie?"

He pressed his hands together. "We've gotta talk."

"We don't have anything to discuss. You're with Mallory."

"That's why I had to find you."

Archie was gonna have to get to the point ASAP. It wasn't like I had unlimited time—especially if he was gonna rub his relationship with Mallory in my face. I had more self-respect than to place myself in a position where I contemplated whether being superficially polite was worth it.

"I don't understand," I said.

"Mallory broke up with me."

"Why would she do that? She lives for hurting me because she can't get over me not liking her."

"Not this time." Archie beamed his eyes at me. "Mallory knows what she did was wrong and has set me free."

"You're lying."

Archie chuckled. "Go ahead. Find Mallory."

No thanks. If I had to choose between associating with Archie and Mallory, I'd choose Archie. I wouldn't have wanted anything to do with Mallory if she rescued me from a burning building.

"So, what?" I asked. "Are we just gonna be together?"

"We could if you want."

I didn't respond. Instead, I scratched an itch on the side of my head. The universe couldn't have handed me a gift. Things didn't happen that easily—even if I intellectualized how I deserved to be happy.

"I'm not angry you were too scared to be with me after you first exposed Mallory's deception," Archie continued.

"How do I know Mallory won't pull something again?" I asked.

Yup. Anyone could say the right thing, but whether Mallory would follow through with her promise was another story. It wasn't like Mallory swore on her mom or dad's grave or on Kelly's life.

Archie swallowed. "You're right—there are no guarantees. But you can't live your life in fear."

"I know, I know."

His cheeks turned bright red while he gritted his teeth. "I'm also sorry for mentioning your father. That wasn't fair of me."

"Thank you for apologizing."

"Please consider giving us another chance." Archie tugged my arm, pulling me against his body. Then, he pressed his lips against my right ear. My pulse soared. I was so close to getting what I wanted, yet I couldn't shake the feeling of my happiness imploding at a moment's notice. When I experienced events such as Dad dying, Mallory's betrayal, or my romantic disappointment with Archie, there was no apologizing for my taking the cautious approach. I was my best advocate.

So, I shoved my skepticism aside despite almost dashing away from Archie. Archie and I stole a glance for the longest time before kissing, even though we were in the school hallway.

Archie's hands drifted from my cheeks to the sides of my head, digging into my hair.

Yeah. Regardless of what the future held, Archie and I would always have this memory. No harm would come from prioritizing my own happiness and tuning out the rest of the world for one fleeting moment.

FRIDAY, SEPTMBER 28, 2018

I sat at one of the tables outside in front of my high school's main entrance, eating lunch.

A slight drizzle pattered against the ground, yet the weather wasn't my biggest priority in life. Minor rain wasn't the end of the world when bigger issues lurked in the back of my mind. Like with Gemma implicating Mallory in whatever happened to Tommy, Archie wanting another chance, or whether Mallory would cause more problems for Archie and me if we reunited.

Footsteps shuffled against the sidewalk, then I lifted my gaze. Great. I so wanted to deal with Mallory.

Mallory cackled. "You've always been a morbid person."

I stood. "I thought you were trying to be a good girl."

"It's only an observation."

"What do you want?" I asked.

"You should try again with Archie. You deserve happiness," Mallory said.

"Interesting." I towered over Mallory—as if false bravado would make this conversation easier. "You could be setting me up only to knock me down. I'm not stupid regardless of how much you hate me."

She huffed out a sigh. "I don't hate you."

"Could've fooled me. You seemed pretty proud of yourself for using Archie to hurt me."

"That was wrong of me, and I wish I could take it back."

"Give me one reason to trust you."

The trees rattled in the wind while Mallory gave me a blink. Perfect. Her silence inspired confidence, and I was wondering if Mallory was figuring out how to continue whatever charade she planned.

"I've got nothing to gain by talking to you." She grabbed a hair tie from her jacket. Then, she ran her fingers through her hair, and placed it in a ponytail. "Not if you're just gonna bite my head off. Besides, you aren't the one I wanna hurt."

I smirked. "Let me guess. Gemma is your target?"

Her jaw shook. "What do you know about her?"

"She has a lot to say about you."

Mallory gripped my hand, and my wrist almost ached. "Tell me everything."

"Let go of me."

"I'm sorry—I shouldn't have grabbed you. That was wrong of me," Mallory said. "But please answer my question."

My gaze narrowed. "She's suspicious of you, so I'd be careful."

"What are you talking about?"

"She thinks you had something to do with Tommy vanishing."

"That's ridiculous," Mallory touted. "Gemma is probably starting trouble to further drive a wedge between us."

There she was. If Mallory wanted me to believe her—even for a moment—then she'd have to continue inflecting the same confidence she just had. Because if Mallory didn't believe what she was saying, then she couldn't expect me to buy her response.

"You've got that covered," I said.

"Ouch."

"I want you to promise me you aren't pulling something with Archie wanting to get back together with me," I said.

Her eyebrows knitted. "I'll do you one better."

"Excuse me?" I asked.

Mallory put her hands on her hips. "Do you hate me so much that you'd give up an opportunity to be happy just to spite me?"

Damn. No matter how close I came to cursing Mallory out, I couldn't say she was wrong—she wasn't. If I wanted to be happy, then I had to ignore the rest of the world like I did when Archie and I had our PDA in the school hallway.

I was about to sit at the table when Mallory hollered at me. "If you're going to believe one thing, then believe my warning about Gemma," she said. "You can't trust her."

"Sure. Whatever you say," I said.

"I'm serious."

"I'm gonna need more than conjecture if you want me to believe you."

Mallory lowered her head. "It's better if you don't know."

Okay. For a second, I almost believed Mallory. Her hatred of Gemma was something that didn't make sense faking, yet the possibility of Mallory's dishonesty loomed in the back of my mind. There was just no telling what I'd get with Mallory—one day she'd be my best friend, and the next she'd put a knife in my back.

So, tension existing between Gemma and Mallory was the only thing I could be certain of. I'd figured out what their bad blood was, though. Having leverage over Mallory was nothing to scoff at.

I almost kicked myself, though. I was no closer to figuring out what I'd do about Archie. Whether I liked the truth or not, I was the one who had to decide what Archie meant to me—not anyone else.

WEDNESDAY, OCTOBER 3, 2018

I scurried through the hallway, heading to cafeteria, only to bump into Gemma.

"My bad," I said.

She pulled her backpack strap higher. "Don't worry; I'm not Mallory. I'm not gonna criticize you for an accident."

I let out a small laugh. "Good to know."

"Looking forward to baking class today?"

"Yeah, making apple pie will be nice. Although I'm bummed, we won't have time to try it till tomorrow."

"Some things are worth waiting for."

"Patience is overrated," I said.

She elevated her eyebrows. "Someone's feeling frisky."

"I'm sorry. I've got a lot on my mind."

"Care to discuss it?" she asked.

"I don't wanna burden you—it's my problem to figure out."

Gemma frowned. "You aren't a burden, Chad, and don't let anyone tell you that."

How considerate of Gemma to take any interest in my life. We were only classmates, and she didn't owe me anything. Especially since Tommy and I stopped being friends a long time ago. Wait. Perhaps Tommy caused Gemma's curiosity into my life.

Whatever. No harm in confiding in Gemma. I might even gain new insight by talking to someone who was neutral. No offense to Rebecca, Dan, or Mom, but they weren't exactly objective. Unlike Gemma, they had a vested interest in my happiness, because they could only deal with me moping around for so long.

"It's Mallory," I mumbled.

"Yeah, she inspires misery."

"I'm serious, she was pretty determined about me giving Archie a second chance."

"What's the problem?" Gemma asked. "Archie's hot, and anyone would kill to date him."

"It feels so convenient."

Gemma took a sip of water before responding. "Has anyone told you never to sabotage your own happiness?"

"It would be different if Mallory never tried to hurt me before," I said.

"True. But I doubt Archie would hurt you."

She had a point. Archie didn't have a reason to hurt me—I hadn't done anything to him. And he probably wouldn't wait around forever. I of all people should've known. I wouldn't have been able to wait the rest of my life for someone to decide if they wanted to be with me. Doing so would've just wasted a lot of time.

"I'm probably overthinking the situation as usual," I said.

She squeezed my hand. "Don't punish yourself—caring is a good thing. Just don't let things fester too long."

"Have you considered being a therapist?" I asked.

"Never. That's the one thing I wouldn't have patience for."

"Don't underestimate yourself," I said.

A couple of girls sporting matching Gucci dresses clipped by us and were soon out of sight. Wow. How nice it must've been to be the Jameson twins. They were juniors like Mallory, Dan, Gemma, Rebecca, and me in addition to how their mother was related to the Vanderbilt family. So, what they wanted, they got.

Gemma tossed her hair behind her shoulders with one flick of her neck, accentuating its dark color. "If you're miserable then that doesn't help you."

"Mallory said the same thing," I said.

She giggled. "For once, she isn't wrong."

"You're absolutely right—I deserve to be happy."

"Fantastic. I'm glad I could help." Gemma peeked at her watch. "Anyway, I have a conference with a teacher, but I'll see you in baking class."

"Thanks again for letting me vent."

"You don't have to thank me for anything, but please be careful. Something unusual is definitely is going on."

"You're gonna have to be more specific."

Gemma cleared her throat. "Tommy's trust fund was completely drained on July 5th—the day before he went missing."

"What are you saying?" I asked.

"Either someone was blackmailing him or he wanted to leave town."

"Have you shared your concerns with the police?"

"My family doesn't exactly gain sympathy, given our wealth. However, I really have to go." Gemma darted down the hallway without another word while the pit in my stomach widened. No matter how challenging my first relationship might be, I owed it to myself not to stew in my own confusion, misery, and worry. If a problem developed, then I'd deal with it then, but not a second sooner—not when I was close to getting everything I wanted.

FRIDAY, OCTOBER 5, 2018

I tapped Archie's back while he stood by his locker, getting the stuff he needed before first period.

He looked into my eyes. "Someone's in a good mood this morning."

Yeah. I wouldn't deny it—I just cracked a smile. For once, I wouldn't let the universe or anything else stand in my way. Not when being proactive about my happiness meant I'd get everything I wanted.

"I was wondering if you had a sec," I said.

"Anything for you."

"I thought about what you said."

"And?" Archie demanded.

"If you're still interested, then I'd like to give things a shot between us."

His smirk expanded. "What makes you think I'd have a better offer so soon?"

I shrugged. "I don't know. There's just no being certain of anything these days. Why? Do you have a better offer?"

Archie elbowed me. "Don't be ridiculous. But yeah, I'd be thrilled to have a fresh start. No drama. Just you, me, and a hotel room to ourselves."

I didn't respond.

"I'm kidding," Archie continued. "We've got plenty of time before we have to worry about that."

"Good."

"Are you gonna kiss me, or what?" he asked.

I pulled Archie in for a quick kiss, and he even gave a little tongue. Yet he did it so subtlety that I didn't feel like a clown was seconds away from molesting me. The embrace continued for another minute, and his hands graced my cheeks, creating brief static from our skin pressing against each other.

My lips twitched after we pulled back from each other, though. Mallory stood at the end of the hallway, and her eyes remained glued on us. Almost as if she might've witnessed my entire interaction with Archie—like the first day of school when Archie and I flirted with each other.

So, yeah. I couldn't be certain of anything—including whether Mallory wanted me to mend my relationship with Archie. The real test of character was when nobody was observing.

Whether I wanted to know what Mallory thought about me when nobody was around could be pushed to another day. For now, Archie was the only thing mattered.

AFTER

MONDAY, DECEMBER 24, 2018

Archie and I stood by his front door.

A thick blanket of snow covered the front lawn, displaying shadows casted by the moonlight. I shivered a little yet couldn't bring myself to say or do anything. In a matter of seconds, I'd meet Archie's parents and sister, and I prayed the evening would go well. It only took one wrong event to ruin a first impression.

He snickered. "Don't tell me your nervous?"

"Wouldn't you feel the same way if you were me?"

"They're going to love you."

"How can you be certain?"

His cheeks flushed. "Because I love you."

Hold on. I might've needed to get my hearing checked. Archie couldn't have said he loved me—not this early in our relationship.

"What's wrong?" he asked.

"You never said that before."

"But it's true. And we've also slept together."

Archie had a point. He hadn't proposed to me—he just told me his feelings. And that wasn't terrible. More honest communication might've saved us drama in the past. Like with Mallory's indecent proposal.

Shit. Everything came back to Mallory no matter what I did or said.

"We should go inside now—we wouldn't want my parents to worry," Archie said.

"One more thing."

He furrowed his eyebrows. "Yes?"

"Is the dinner gonna be awkward because of Mallory revealing your father's unemployment?"

"That doesn't matter."

I blinked. "It doesn't?"

"Nope. He found a new job as a VP at another advertising firm, so don't panic."

Maybe, just maybe, I should've been a little more grateful. For once, the universe wasn't against me, and that fact should've been cherished. Whether I accepted the truth or not, problems occasionally resolved themselves.

He laughed louder this time. "Enough stalling. My parents must be worried about us."

"I've gotta say another thing."

"I never knew you had such a big mouth."

"Thank you for driving me to your house even though I have a car," I said.

He pushed my chin up. "You don't need to thank me for anything—that's what boyfriends are for."

Boyfriends. The word surpassed the beauty from a church's stained-glass window. Something nice existed from getting my way for once in my life. No matter how cynical I might've been, I couldn't deny how life would be easier if every day wasn't such a struggle. There was no point to living if I'd never be able to have fun.

Wind swooshed through the air, scattering snow on the front lawn before stinging our faces. Yikes. The weather was colder than I imagined.

"Come on." Archie grabbed my hand, then we entered his home and went to the living room.

Three buckets of champagne rested on the living room table, and a man, woman, and girl—who was probably only a couple of years younger than Archie and I sat on the beige couch. I couldn't stop thinking about the champagne. I wasn't sure if the goal was to get better acquainted or party like it was New Year's Eve.

The woman rose before clapping her hands together. "We almost sent a search party for you."

No offense to Archie's mother, but melodrama wasn't necessary. Archie and I were entitled to steal a moment for ourselves. Doing so was the least we deserved after every twist and turn in our lives since the beginning of the school year. It wasn't like we were that late. Probably only ten or fifteen minutes at best.

"Great to meet you." Archie's mother hugged me before I could respond with a greeting, and my breathing picked up a little.

Whatever. Not a big deal if his mother liked firm hugs—there were bigger things to get upset about. Like if my friends and I would go to jail because of the Tommy situation.

"Anyway, please call me Doreen," she said after releasing me from my hug.

I gave her a quick look over. The ugly Santa sweater and jeans might've indicated that she wasn't uptight—I didn't expect a parent to dress so casually during the first meeting of the boyfriend—yet something needed to be done about her hair. Her blonde lowlights and highlights resembled stripes.

Archie's father stood next. "I'm George. Nice to meet you."

George extended his hand and I took it. Except my hand almost detached from my arm, begging the question: Did George and Doreen care about hospitality or were they without qualms about killing their guests within the first couple minutes of meeting them?

Archie's sister hugged me before I could catch my breath. Her greeting wasn't like a python wrapping its body around me, yet she kept rubbing my back. Almost as if she might've been feeling me up.

Archie removed his sister from me. "That's enough Andrea."

"I wanted to see what the fuss is about." Andrea tossed her hair over her shoulder, emphasizing its color. Her hair was blonde like mine, except she had pink streaks. "You also said he's bisexual like you."

"Let's keep the dinner G-rated," George said.

Andrea pouted. "Don't be a buzzkill."

Doreen squealed. "I've got an idea. How about we open some champagne?"

"But we aren't twenty-one," I said.

Andrea jabbed my shoulder. "I didn't you realize you were as uptight as my father. Perhaps I can help with that."

"Save your sex crazed fantasies for boarding school," Archie said.

"Doesn't matter if you three are underage," Doreen said, pointing to Andrea, Archie, and I. "Christmas Eve is a special occasion and I won't be burdened by an arbitrary drinking age. You can also stay the night if you don't feel like going home."

Andrea's eyes lit up brighter than the Christmas tree a few feet away from us. "I'd love it if Chad stayed the night."

"In your dreams," Archie said.

Andrea giggled. "I've never had a threesome before."

Doreen almost dropped the flute glass when she handed it to me. "Andrea, please!"

"I'm trying to lighten the mood," Andrea said.

"Nobody asked for your commentary," Archie said.

"Let's not fight," George said.

Archie glared at his sister. "It's a miracle you haven't been kicked out of boarding school. What were your grades this past semester?"

"My teachers have till January 3rd to upload the semester grades," Andrea said.

"Likely story," Archie said.

Doreen raised her glass. "Not even Andrea's bad grades can spoil the evening, because I propose a toast. You've got no idea how nice it is to finally meet you, Chad."

I glanced at Archie. "You've mentioned me?"

How exciting. I hadn't once considered that Archie might've discussed me with his family. I just assumed Archie was like me and spent most of his time hoping we wouldn't be exposed for the Tommy situation.

"Only a couple of times," Archie said.

Andrea adjusted her dress, accentuating her boobs. "Don't be modest. You should've seen him this morning at breakfast, Chad. He gave us an hour speech about how he'd disown us if we fucked up this evening."

"Language!" George exclaimed.

"Get your stick out of your ass, Dad," Andrea said. "Because I already have."

George spat out his champagne, then Doreen handed him a napkin. He dunked it in a nearby water glass before wetting his shirt. But he didn't speak. Instead, the shade of red dotting his cheeks grew brighter.

Doreen turned to her daughter. "What did I say about having more discretion?"

"I don't know; I wasn't paying attention," Andrea said.

I leaned into Archie's ear. "Your family is rather colorful."

"Don't remind me," Archie said.

"Don't worry about it." I sipped my champagne. The mixture of the sweet, tart, and carbonated flavors electrified my taste buds while the beverage lingered in my mouth for a beat before swallowing it. "I've got a lot of material for a new short story."

"You better change the names," Archie said.

"If you're lucky," I said.

Doreen drew in a breath. "I'll give you five hundred dollars if you behave yourself for the rest of the evening, Andrea."

Andrea didn't even stroke her chin. "Fine. But I want it in cash."

I wouldn't chastise Andrea for her behavior no matter how much I almost cringed. Moments like these provided more relief than a monsoon in a desert. Borderline inappropriate relatives were the greatest problem I should've dealt with—not a murder situation, which had the power to send me to prison for the rest of my life. I also knew the difference between Andrea and someone with malicious intentions—she was only a harmless flirt who'd move onto the next guy in a matter of time.

WEDNESDAY, DECEMBER 26, 2018

I exited Starbucks sometime in the afternoon, gripping my caramel macchiato, only to bump into Gemma.

She smiled. "Belated Merry Christmas."

"You too."

"Did you have a good Christmas?"

"Yes. What about you?"

"It was great," Gemma said.

I inhaled sharply. Even an innocent conversation with Gemma could be problematic. Watching what I said was my only option when there was no telling what Gemma was planning. Like if Gemma knew Tommy had still been alive and planned on leaving town after Tommy got the money from Mallory.

So, I only had one option. Scurry away from Gemma before she could probe the Tommy issue and make me admit something terrible.

She cackled. "What's the hurry?"

"I have to do grocery shopping—I promised my mother I'd cook dinner."

"It won't kill you to chat for several minutes. We're baking buddies. Or do you no longer care about how we used to be partners in baking class?"

"I've got a lot on my mind."

Gemma folded her arms. "I can imagine."

"And what's that supposed to mean?"

"I'm not stupid. You and your friends are hiding something about Tommy and I'm gonna find out what it is."

I pursed my lips. "I don't know what you're talking about."

"Save it. Tommy and I were planning on leaving town the night of the Snowflake Ball once he got the money from Mallory. What I don't know is where Tommy disappeared to. But don't worry, because I'm gonna uncover the truth if it's the last thing I do." Gemma's hair smacked her in the face after wind rippled through the air.

"All you've got is conjecture," I said.

"It's not conjecture if it's true."

I arched my eyebrows. "What do you want from me?"

"There's no reason for you to go down. Mallory is the only one I'm after."

"I guess forgiveness would've been too much for you."

She put her hands in her coat pockets. "Kindness is overrated—punishment is much more enjoyable."

Wow. Despite all my interactions with Gemma, I hadn't once pondered that she might've been as bitter about Mallory as me. Perhaps it was because a small part of me wanted to believe the best in Mallory no matter much we feuded. The alternative would've been too grim because I didn't know what I would've done if I admitted my friendship with Mallory was over forever.

"It's not your job to punish people," I said.

"I disagree."

The wind roared even louder this time, pushing a crushed can down the sidewalk. So much for people caring about littering in this town.

Gemma and I just continued staring at each other. I wasn't sure what I'd say at this point, because I had to regain the upper hand in the conversation. Even if it meant throwing something in her face—something that would've turned the entire world against her. Whether I had the guts to mention said fact was another thing. There was no taking back what I said once I revealed I knew about her and Tommy.

Fuck it. Whether it Gemma, Mallory, or anyone else, I wouldn't be pushed around. Not this time. It wasn't like I wanted to harm Gemma. She just needed to know I wasn't someone to be trifled with.

"I know about your relationship with Tommy," I blurted.

Her jaw lowered. "I'm not gonna apologize for that."

"What? You aren't even gonna deny your relationship with Tommy?" I asked.

"No point in wasting time."

"You didn't answer my question. What do you want from me?"

"Help me destroy Mallory. Anyone can see how she's still a threat to your relationship with Archie," Gemma said.

My heart fluttered. I couldn't accuse Gemma of being soft. Her comment enticed me more than it should've. Mallory and I could pretend to be friends all we wanted, but I'd never lie to myself concerning my relationship with Archie. I'd always wonder if Mallory would ruin my relationship with him once we got passed the Tommy situation.

"What if I told you I knew what happened to Tommy?" I asked.

Yeah. No harm in teasing what I knew — I had time to decide whether I'd actually reveal to Gemma everything that happened the night Tommy died.

"I'd be interested," she said.

"I'm only gonna tell you this because you've got no way to prove it."

Gemma made a tsk-tsk sound. "I meant what I said. I have no interest in hurting you. Alienating the one person who hates Mallory as much as I do would be a mistake. It's not like I'm wearing a wire or have a tape recorder."

Perhaps the CIA should've recruited Gemma. She might've been what the agency needed when recruiting assets. If I didn't know better, then I couldn't deny that Gemma went out of her way to reassure me of whom I could trust. Almost as if she wasn't lying and wanted Mallory gone as much as I did.

"Tommy was gonna kill me because Mallory didn't have the money, but Mallory saved my life," I said.

"I assume Archie was with you two. I saw him and Mallory hanging out a lot before the Snowflake Ball."

Apparently, the universe wasn't in the mood to protect. I would've kept Archie out of the situation in a perfect world, yet I couldn't deny his involvement.

"Yes," I mumbled.

"Relax. I'm also not interested in hurting Archie either," Gemma said. "Tell me something else. Do Rebecca and Dan know about the situation?"

I nodded. "Yes."

"They aren't a target either."

"You really wanna destroy Mallory over an accident?" I asked.

"She deserves it. If it's not this, then it'd be over something else. Look at this way, I'm doing the world a favor."

"I still haven't decided if I wanna help."

"I'm a generous person, so I'll give you some time, but not too much." Gemma strutted down the block without another word.

Wow. How nice it must've been to be Gemma—I would've given my life savings never to have worry about anything again. Most people would've danced around their intentions. But no. Gemma made her declaration, and that was that. The only question was if I'd go along with her plan. Never seeing Mallory again offered more appeal than an impromptu trip to Hawaii, yet I still went back to my earlier point no matter how much Mallory sinned against me. A tiny part of me would've gone into a fetal position if my friendship with Mallory ended. Losses that didn't involve death were sometimes the most difficult situations to move on from—at least death provided closure.

FRIDAY, DECEMBER 28, 2018

Mallory and I sat at a table in back of Café Tomorrow.

She pushed the chipped mug towards me. "I ordered for you because I'd bet my life on you wanting a hot caramel macchiato."

"Nothing is worth betting your life for."

"We'll agree to disagree."

Her gaze remained on her cup. Wow. She still hadn't made eye contact with me since I arrived a couple minutes ago, and I could only speculate about what bombshell she'd drop on me.

"Just tell me whatever is on your mind," I said. "You know I'll find out eventually, so save us time."

Yeah. Even I could be generous with Mallory after everything she did for me. And my reasoning wasn't even because she saved my life. Nope. It was still the holiday season, and I could spare some generosity as long as Mallory didn't take advantage.

She coughed, then looked upward. "I owe you an apology."

"I don't follow."

"I never dealt with my parents dying and then Tommy's betrayal was the final push. So, that's why I've been the way I am."

"You're gonna have to elaborate," I said.

"Kelly saw a grief counselor after my parents, but I didn't." Mallory pouted. "That's why I've used you as a target for my anger—like when you rejected me at the beginning of the school year. It wasn't because I admired Glenn Close's character in *Fatal Attraction*. It was because I'm sick of everything going wrong. But I know I can't keep acting the same way and expect different results. I've had my first few sessions with a therapist, and it's already doing miracles for me."

"I lost a parent as well, but I didn't turn into a jerk."

She exhaled deeply. "I'm not trying to justify my behavior. I just want you to know it didn't come out of nowhere."

"Why be honest now?"

Mallory patted my hand. "Uniting together is the only way we're gonna survive the Tommy situation. Especially if Gemma might already be suspicious of us."

Gemma. There that name was again. I so loved how Mallory brought her up. It wasn't like I hadn't thought about Gemma 5,000 times. I was fully aware her generosity wouldn't last forever. Eventually, Gemma would want a decision. And I'd have to figure out if I could live with hurting Mallory like she hurt me.

"This can't be easy for you," I said.

"Doesn't matter. It was important."

I sipped my caramel macchiato. "Perhaps we'll be able to get along now."

"I hope so, because I meant what I said. I've got nothing to gain by lying. Not when we could lose everything."

How great for me. Mallory's character change happened at the least opportune time. No matter how much I wanted to believe she wanted to be a better person, I couldn't shake the memory of her facial expression when she spied on my first conversation with Archie. Or the time she snuck into my bedroom in hopes of me stopping my investigation about the Tommy situation.

So, yeah. I had a lot to think about now, and I was just thrilled. My life would always get more complicated, not less complicated.

SATURDAY, DECEMBER 29, 2018

My head remained on Archie's chest while he ran his fingers through my hair, stroking it. We were fully clothed and lay on top of my bed comforter. Even if I couldn't tell Archie about Gemma's offer, I could still be close to him.

"Do you believe what Mallory told you?" he asked.

"Yes. She has no reason to lie."

"But do you actually trust her?"

Just because Archie couldn't know about my conversation with Gemma didn't mean I couldn't tell him about my feelings for Mallory. Like how I could make her mad without realizing it, only for her to scheme against me—even if Mallory might've been seeing a therapist and believed she was being a better person.

Crap. My head spun because of all this thinking. No matter how many times I considered the possibilities, I couldn't predict the future.

"No," I finally said.

"Then you've got your answer."

BEFORE

MONDAY, OCTOBER 8, 2018

I closed my locker after getting everything I needed for first period, only to be greeted by hands covering my eyes.

No need for an increased heartbeat, though. The deodorant wafting through the air revealed who stood behind me, so I wouldn't alert the FBI about a serial striking again.

"Hi," Archie said.

"What's up?"

"I thought we could chat before first period."

"Sure. Anything on your mind?" I asked.

"There's something I wanted to ask you."

I scrunched my eyebrows. "Everything okay?"

"Yeah, it's nothing bad."

I laughed. "Good. You know how I feel about surprises."

"I was wondering if you'd want to go out on a date."

I blinked. "Really?"

He nudged my shoulder. "Why is that so hard to believe?"

Truthfully, Archie was right. There shouldn't have been anything complicated about our first date. Yet I couldn't forget about the universe. Like wondering when the next bad thing would happen. Pushing my pride aside and giving my relationship with Archie a real chance didn't mean I forgot about Mallory—I hadn't. I couldn't. And the small possibility of Mallory doing something bad lurked in my mind.

"You're right. A date sounds lovely," I said.

He wagged his finger at me. "I hope you know it's okay to be happy."

"What did you have in mind?" I asked.

Archie shrugged. "I don't know. I'd thought we could discuss it—I didn't wanna be presumptuous about what your favorite food is."

Wow. His response indicated we were possibly meant for each other. There was nothing worse than someone making an assumption. Like if he assumed I was okay with spicy food—that wouldn't be a good way to beginning our relationship.

"It's a tie between Chinese and Italian," I said.

Archie chuckled, yet didn't respond. And I couldn't help raising my eyebrows—I hadn't said anything funny.

"Sorry," he said. "I'm not teasing you. It's just those are my favorite foods, and I hate when someone makes me choose between the two."

The glee radiating from my smile wasn't an overreaction. Just because the universe always screwed me over, didn't mean I wished life was difficult. I didn't. And if that happened from sharing the same taste in food as Archie, then so be it. Sometimes, the little things were what got me through the day.

"When did you wanna go out?" I asked.

"That was another thing I wanted to check with you."

"I'm free any night this week or we could do the weekend if you wanted."

Archie ruffled his hair. "Either works for me."

Lilac scented perfume trickled through the air, and I craned my neck. Mallory just strutted down the hallway. Her presence didn't concern me, though. Her attitude is what tingled my spine. Whether intentional or not, Mallory once again sported her hyena grin. The kind of expression that revealed she might've been planning something.

Unless my concern was in my head—that wasn't impossible. A difference existed between pursuing a guy to spite me and going on a shooting spree. Hmmm. If I wanted to be happy, then maybe I'd have to believe happiness was possible. Like that mantra, mind over matter. Doing so was worth a shot—life couldn't get any worse.

"What are you thinking about?" Archie demanded.

"Nothing important."

He folded his arms. "Like I believe you."

Good for him. Archie could've been a detective. The no bullshit approach would've made him perfect for the police academy.

I looped my arms around his neck, then gazed into his eyes. "I'm thinking about how epic our date will be."

"Sure. Whatever you say."

Yup. No regret necessary for fibbing to Archie. People didn't want to admit morality was sometimes complicated, but it was. If fudging the truth helped me sleep at night, then so be it. Mallory didn't need to join this conversation—whether physically or just by name.

"Let's change the topic," Archie continued. "Have you been on a date before?"

"No," I said without looking away.

He winked. "Then that makes you a virgin."

I wrinkled my nose. "Very funny."

WEDNESDAY, OCOTBER 10, 2018

Archie and I turned the corner in the school hallway, only for him to give me a quick peck on the lips.

"I'm sorry I can't have lunch with you, but my English conference awaits," he said.

"No worries—I'll survive. And it'll be fun to catch up with Rebecca and Dan."

"You could pretend to miss me."

I tapped his nose. "Very funny. But don't be late for your meeting. You know Mrs. Bell will kill you if you're even five seconds late."

Archie kissed me one more time, then darted down the hallway. I didn't move from my current location. Not having my insides filled with dread for once in my life provided more joy than I could've ever imagined. Maybe my words from the other day were true: I needed to believe happiness was possible if I wanted to be happy.

Someone cackled and my back hairs rose. The noise was worse than someone dragging their fingernails across a chalkboard.

The girl standing by the water fountain trekked over to me.

"What do you want, Mallory?" I asked.

"Is that anyway to greet a friend?"

"We aren't friends."

She gritted her teeth. "Why? Because of a couple conversations you had with Gemma? She isn't perfect either."

"It's not about that and you know it."

"Looks like you got everything you wanted, so you've got nothing to complain about."

"I don't report to you and can think or feel whatever I want," I said.

The bell rang. Hopefully, Archie made it to his writing conference—I wasn't joking about Mrs. Bell being more uptight than someone who had been constipated for a month. She once gave someone a detention for an excused absence. Dwelling on Archie and Mrs. Bell might've also helped me get rid of Mallory. If she saw I wasn't interested in chatting—not even about the weather—then she might leave me alone.

Mallory grabbed a strand of her hair. "You and Archie look happy."

"That's none of your business."

"Relax. I'll give you points for consistency," she said.

"There's something you should know." I undid the top button of my polo shirt. Somehow, the hallway spun around me and sweat dripped down my back despite how the school hadn't cranked on the heat yet. "I'm not afraid of you, so give it your best shot."

"What are you talking about?" Mallory asked.

"It doesn't take a Harvard student to know you're plotting something big."

So much for a positive mental attitude because no matter how nice living in a world without drama would've been, I still had to protect myself. Even if doing so entailed inventing problems that didn't exist yet. Luring someone into a false sense of security was the exact thing someone did right before making a final play for revenge.

Her lips twitched. "Careful, Chad. Paranoia doesn't look good on you."

"It's not paranoia if it's real."

"I'm not a threat to your relationship with Archie. But maybe you'd see that if you weren't so judgmental."

Okay. Time for a reality check.

I snorted. "Have you forgotten what you did?"

"That's in the past. Besides, I've got other things to focus on."

"Maybe I should tell Kelly what you did. I'm sure she won't be happy to learn people are just dolls to you."

"That's not true, and you know it," Mallory snapped, her face turning scarlet.

Several students flocked down the hallway, and I remained silent. Causing a scene before I graduated high school wasn't exactly on the top of my priority list.

I scoffed. "Actions speak louder than words."

"Where'd you get that? On the back of a Hallmark card?"

"And you wonder why I don't want anything to do with you," I said.

She locked her hands together. "You're right. If I want you to trust me, then I should give you a reason to."

"Go on."

"I want you to be happy regardless of whether you can ever be friends with me again."

"Interesting," I said.

Mallory drew in a breath. "I'm serious. Have you forgotten I understand what losing a parent is like?"

When Mallory was right, she was right. No matter how much I wanted to prove her to wrong, I couldn't forget about her parents dying. Surely, that caused all her current behavioral problems. Generalizations were sometimes true no matter how much people might've fought against them. With Mallory, that meant she might've wanted a target for anger. Even if it was her former best friend.

"It's not my fault a drunk driver killed your parents," I said.

She grumbled. "I never said it was."

We continued standing in silence. If Mallory wanted me to consider being friends with her someday in a vague, distant future, then she had to work for it.

"Have you and Archie gone out on a date yet?" she asked.

Deep breaths. Maybe I had a third option that didn't involve forgiving her or never speaking to her again. I could try making small talk—even if it was about Archie. It wasn't impossible for us to be friends again after enough time passed, or at least we could be friendlier towards each other. No matter how justified the anger pulsing through my body was, life shouldn't have been so hard.

I coughed. "Not yet, but we will at some point this week. We're just trying to decide what to do."

"If you wanna bounce ideas off me, I'd be happy to listen."

FRIDAY, OCTOBER 12, 2018

Waves crashed into the sand while the stench of salty sea water lingered in the air.

"I hope this wasn't a dumb idea." Archie shifted his weight on the beach towel next to me, making eye contact.

"No need to apologize." I took several slices of salami from the basket between us. "A picnic is a great idea for a first date."

"Even if Crescent Beach is haunted?" he asked.

I rolled my eyes. "That's an urban legend."

"Don't be so skeptical."

"I'll believe it when I see it."

He snickered. "A ghost sighting would be quite the first date."

I poked his elbow. "Don't even think it. Ghosts are like Green Eggs and Ham. I don't want them anywhere."

"Really?" Archie sipped his champagne. "A writer should be more adventurous."

"There's only so much I'm willing to do in the name of art."

"Live a little."

Interesting. I wouldn't have expected Archie to be a daredevil. Then again, I was still getting to know him.

Sunlight continued beaming from the sky, and I squinted. "Damn. I should've brought my sunglasses," I said.

Archie handed me his shades. "Have mine."

How kind of him. He hadn't even given the issue a second thought. I couldn't even dream of being so kind. Not when I was never certain of what the universe had planned for me.

"You need them." I grabbed the champagne bottle from the picnic basket, poured myself a more than generous serving, then sipped it. This brand of champagne wasn't too dry or too sweet. However, Archie hadn't told me how he procured the champagne—so I didn't know if he took the bottle from his parents' wine cellar or if he had a fake ID and went to a liquor store that didn't hassle minors. A little mystery might've been okay, though. A first date with Archie felt like a controlled environment compared with other situations where I'd cringe from anticipating what life had planned for me.

"It's okay. I want you to have them."

Okay. If he really felt that way, I'd take them. Whether Archie realized the point or not, he just provided fodder for a new short story.

Giving a jacket to a date was the chivalrous thing to do, but nobody ever considered squinting, so I had a fresh twist to an old trope.

Archie stretched his feet out on the towel. "Something funny?"

"No. Everything is good."

"Have you thought about forgiving Mallory?" he asked.

Hold on. Archie couldn't have just mentioned Mallory. There was no acceptable reason for mentioning her. Especially if Archie and I hadn't kissed yet.

"I'm not trying to upset you," Archie continued. "However, I ran into her in the hallway the other day and she mentioned you had a nice conversation."

Funny. I wouldn't have labeled my conversation with Mallory nice, but that was just me. I'd never stop looking out for myself. We still had a long way to go before I'd consider mending our friendship.

"I should show you one of my short stories at some point," I said.

"Fine. I can take a hint." He grabbed the champagne bottle, only to shake his head. Apparently, the alcohol went quicker than expected—even if it was only the two of us as opposed to a college party.

I wiped my eye. "I should thank you."

"For what?"

"Waiting for me. Most guys would grow impatient."

"That's easy." He batted his eyes, then leaned forward. Our lips were now less than inch from each other. "You're worth it."

"Smart answer."

"I was gonna wait till I dropped you at home but fuck it." Archie grabbed my shirt collar before kissing me. His hands traveled up my neck to my cheeks. After that, I slipped out of my leather jacket. There wasn't even a faint chill in the air, so I shouldn't have been so zealous with my wardrobe—I was the guy who sported shorts in winter.

Whether either one of us discussed Mallory again during our date didn't matter, though. We had the beach to ourselves, so seizing the opportunity for making out was our only concern. Life might not have been perfect, yet somehow the universe handed me another picturesque moment to hold onto, and I'd take it. No telling when the opportunity would arise again.

SATURDAY, OCTOBER 13, 2018

Rebecca and I sat at a table in front of Café Tomorrow—the air still hadn't reached its vindictive, lung-stinging coldness—while a pigeon nibbled on something poking out from a nearby garbage can before flying away.

"Thanks for this." She blew on her coffee, then sipped it. "Being a loser and eating by myself wouldn't have been fun."

"Good to know I'm the backup."

She glared at me. "Don't be like that. It's not my fault Dan forgot he had a tutoring session today."

Interesting. Perhaps I wasn't the only one who couldn't take a joke.

"Don't worry about it. Having someone to dissect my date with is the perfect way to spend my morning." I broke off part of my croissant before dunking it in my coffee.

She clapped her hand over her mouth. "That's right! I forgot about you and Archie. How was it?"

No need for her dramatics. We were discussing romance, not a terminal cancer diagnosis. So, Rebecca could save her theatrics for when someone casted her in an Oscar winning role.

I smirked. "Let's just say last night is the closest I've ever come to having sex on a beach."

"Good for you—I'm impressed."

"Thanks."

"Are you gonna have a second date?" Rebecca asked.

My jaw didn't even shudder. "Absolutely."

"Good." She finished her remaining coffee, then pushed her mug to the side. "But there's something we need to discuss."

Perfect. Nothing to ruin the morning like a phrase that resembled a blaring siren—I deserved a few minutes of pleasure before speculating about when the next annoying thing would occur.

"Yes?" I forced out.

"I don't blame you for how you feel about Mallory, but you need to let your anger go," she said. "It's not healthy."

No offense to Rebecca, but it wasn't her job to determine what was and wasn't healthy. I was entitled to my feelings, so she should've saved her breath.

"What? Do you wanna be friends with her?" I asked.

"No, but you're never gonna be happy if you're so consumed about what Mallory is planning next."

I sighed. "Enough about me. I'd rather talk about you and Dan."

"Not so fast. What I'm saying is important."

Okay, Mom. If she wanted to resemble a parent, then so be it. I couldn't do anything to change her mind if she remained intent on lecturing me.

She patted my hand. "I only want nice things for you."

"I know, I know."

"I'm serious. This kind of energy isn't healthy."

"She took Archie from me twice," I said, raising my voice.

"That's over with."

Easy for her to say. Dan wasn't the one with wandering eyes. It wasn't that I thought Archie would cheat on me—I just couldn't forget about all of his interactions with Mallory. Manipulating Archie wasn't the same as putting a gun to his head—only a fool would've thought Archie didn't enjoy spending time with Mallory.

MONDAY, OCTOBER 15, 2018

I rounded the corner in the school hallway on my way to baking class, only to bump into Gemma.

"Wanna walk to class together?" she asked.

"Fine by me."

We clipped down the remainder hallway before turning left and shuffling down another corridor. But I didn't speak. Not when my conversation with Rebecca still weighed on my mind. She should've known better than to tell me how to feel and think. Even if she didn't have malicious intentions. I would've liked to see how she would've reacted if someone threatened her relationship with Dan.

Gemma tilted her head. "Something wrong?"

"Doesn't matter."

She halted before touching my arm. "If something is bothering you, then please tell me."

"Just about Mallory."

"Did she do something?"

"Not yet, but it doesn't change my gut instincts," I said.

"Always go with your intuition."

My shoulders tensed. "It's not like I'm having a psychotic break."

She giggled. "Don't apologize for your feelings."

"If Mallory proves me wrong, then great. But I'm not clueless," I said.

"It'd be nice to get an answer about what's going on." Gemma flicked the hair stuck in her jacket behind her shoulder. "My parents are still livid about Tommy's trust fund being raided before he disappeared."

I furrowed my brow. "Mallory said your parents weren't too distraught about Tommy's absence."

"She's lying," Gemma said, voice cracking. "They've had more than one sleepless night concerning Tommy."

"And the trust fund?"

Gemma scanned the hallway—no teachers or students were within earshot. "Money doesn't disappear into thin air for no reason. It's not like Tommy had to go to someone for access to it. The trust fund was linked to his bank account, and he only needed his debit card."

"What are you saying?" I asked.

"I'm still convinced Mallory had something to do with Tommy vanishing," she said.

Whether or not Gemma's hunch was correct, I couldn't shake her comment about the money. That was something tangible, and it might be a clue. And I couldn't forget about the lying. Being dishonest about something that was verifiable wasn't smart—it seemed like Mallory got sloppy. But the implications from what Gemma said were another thing. Speculating was all I could do until I discovered more answers.

AFTER

TUESDAY, JANUARY 15, 2019

I shuffled through the school hallway on the way to lunch, only to cross paths with Gemma.

She put her hands on her hips. "You haven't given me an answer."

"I've had a lot on my mind."

"Don't bullshit me—you're avoiding me."

"I need time to decide what I want to do."

Gemma pulled me aside when a couple of other students flocked by. "There's nothing to ponder. Mallory is a bitch and deserves to be destroyed."

Perhaps Mallory wasn't the only one who needed counseling. If Gemma wasn't careful, then she might explode in front of the wrong person. And that would be great—especially if said person was me. Having two unhinged people in my life was my dream, and I couldn't have been more grateful if I tried.

"It must be lonely being you," I said.

"I can live with loneliness if I get justice for Tommy."

"Why not go to the police?" I asked.

"What I have in my mind is much worse than the police could ever do"

Good to know I wasn't on Gemma's shit-list. I didn't wanna consider what she would've done to me if I pissed her off.

I elevated my eyebrows. "You really think it's your job to get justice?"

"Somebody has to keep people honest," Gemma said.

I sighed. "Mallory has been trying to become a better person."

"I find that hard to believe." Gemma scoffed. "What did she do? Help an old lady cross the street?"

"I'm serious, Gemma. She's been seeing a therapist to deal with her parents dying."

Her eyes widened. "You believe her?"

"I checked with Kelly—it's true."

"What if Kelly's lying?"

"She has no reason to extend herself for Mallory—they've never gotten along."

She grumbled. "Who cares if she's trying to be a better person? She's the reason Tommy died, so that makes her a terrible person."

Yikes. Gemma wasn't just slightly unhinged—she was committed to this whole revenge thing. And I had another reason to stay awake at night. Her tenacity and determination suggested she wouldn't stop till she got what she wanted. A chill rolled up my back. There were a thousand possibilities of what Gemma's revenge could entail, and each scenario was worse than the previous one.

"But it was to protect me," I said.

"Stop making excuses for her." Gemma pushed a chunk of her hair to the side. "Mallory would've found another reason for killing Tommy if you weren't involved in the situation."

I swallowed the lump in my throat. "You don't blame me for Tommy's death?"

"No!" Gemma exclaimed. "And please don't make me repeat myself again. I've got a mission, and I'm not gonna stop till Mallory gets what's coming to her."

"I want more time."

"For what?" Gemma asked. "Divine intervention? Mallory is never gonna change who she is, and the sooner you accept that fact the better."

"How can you be so cold?"

"I'm not the monster everyone thinks I am," Gemma said.

"I find that hard to believe. You've done nothing to give me a positive impression of you."

"I'm letting you and your friends off the hook for covering up Tommy's murder."

"You can turn on me any moment," I said.

"Fine." She grunted so loud I almost thought the teachers that just passed us would glare, but they didn't. Instead, Gemma rolled up her sleeve. A pink streak on her lower arm became visible, and I almost literally bit my tongue. No matter how twisted the universe was, it always found a way for me to think it was worse. "My father did this to me when I was twelve. Something about me needing to learn children shouldn't talk until spoken to."

"I'm so sorry."

"I don't care what anyone else thinks of me—Tommy and I did what we needed to survive."

"Sleeping with your brother provided the comfort you needed?" I asked.

"You make it sound worse than it is."

I chuckled. "That's incest."

"Call it whatever you want. All I know is that Tommy was the love of my life, and Mallory took him from me."

"I met your father once after chatting with your mother about Tommy. He was something else, but I never thought he was abusive," I said.

"Count yourself lucky you never saw how evil he really was."

Once I made a decision about helping Gemma, there was no going back. So, yeah. Whether I thought about the point once or a million times didn't matter. I had to make sure I'd be okay with whatever decision I reached. Regret was about the only feeling that surpassed betrayal.

"Anyway, you have one week," Gemma said.

"Excuse me?"

"I'm serious. I want an answer by end of the school day on Tuesday January 22nd or you and your friends might go down with Mallory."

"You wouldn't do that," I said.

"Maybe. Maybe not. But you don't wanna test me." Gemma threw her backpack over her shoulder, then trekked down the hallway.

Decisions. Decisions.

I could either forgive Mallory or not. But I couldn't keep vacillating—the ambiguity wasn't healthy and would only cause more dark circles under my eyes. I should've asked Gemma what her plan entailed, though. Scheming was one thing, yet I couldn't help her if she planned on physically harming Mallory—violence was one step too far. I could at least pretend to have principles.

WEDNESDAY, JANUARY 16, 2019

I planned on baking brownies after school while Mom was at yoga, yet the doorbell rang several times. And I'd pray I didn't have to deal with an impromptu visit from Gemma—I had six more days before I had to make a decision.

My shoulders tensed upon opening the front door.

Gemma wasn't the reason for blinking several times, though. Sunlight glinted against gold badges attached to both the man and woman's belts.

"Can I help you?" I asked.

The woman offered her hand. "I'm Bonnie Jones, and this is my partner Skip Garrison. We're with the local police department and would like to ask you some questions about Tommy Drake."

"Should I be talking with you? My mother isn't home," I said.

"You aren't a person of interest, so we aren't breaking any rules." Detective Garrison rubbed his mustache, which covered every spec of skin above his lip. "Unless you've got something to hide."

Detective Jones nudged her partner. "What did I tell you about being more personable? You're never gonna get promoted if your reputation doesn't improve."

Slamming the door in their faces tempted me for a split second. I wasn't a suspect and avoiding them would be easier. But I also watched my fair share of *Law and Order* reruns, so I wouldn't have done anything to attract attention—even if someone paid a billion dollars.

I gesticulated at them. "Please come inside."

They entered my home, and I closed the door behind them.

"Can I get you anything? Tea? Coffee? Soda? Water?" I asked.

Detective Garrison groaned. "This isn't a social call."

"You'll have to excuse my partner," Detective Jones said. "He's having an off month and forgot his manners. He meant to say refreshments won't be necessary since we're here on official police business."

Detective Garrison adjusted his tie. "More like an off year."

"Okay. What can I do for you?" I asked.

"We know you were friends with Mallory," Detective Jones replied.

"Yeah, I was. But I'm not quite sure how that fact is relevant," I said.

"We were wondering if you could provide insight into Mallory and Tommy's relationship? Were they happy?" Detective Jones said.

I raised my eyebrows. "What kind of insight?"

Just because my pulse didn't reverberate in my ears didn't mean I couldn't be careful. I wouldn't give them extra information. Not when my entire future could be ripped away from me at a moment's notice.

"Did they ever argue?" Detective Jones asked.

"Is Mallory a suspect?" I asked.

"We can't comment on an ongoing investigation," Detective Garrison spat.

Detective Jones giggled. "Lighten up, Skip. Some honesty might encourage Chad to be truthful with us. It'd be hypocritical to expect his cooperation and be totally clammed up about the investigation."

"Just trying to do things by the book," Detective Garrison said.

Go Detective Jones! If didn't know better, then I would've suspected she was best friends with Archie's sister, Andrea. Andrea would've had no problem breaking protocol if she was a cop.

"Rules are overrated," Detective Jones said.

I snickered. Might as well have found a little humor in the situation if I couldn't figure out what their agenda was.

"Could you answer my question?" I asked.

"Yes." Detective Jones gripped her ponytail where it was laying across her shoulder. "Mallory is a person of interest in the case, so if you know anything—even something that might seem irrelevant—then don't hesitate to tell us. It's our job to put the pieces together."

"I'm afraid I don't have much to tell you. Mallory and Tommy seemed happy," I said.

Detective Garrison stared me down. "That's an interesting response."

I shrugged. "What? Do you want me to lie and say they were the perfect couple?"

"No," Detective Jones said, throwing a gaze over her shoulder. "We don't want you to be phony with us."

"I'm sure their relationship had problems like any other couple, but I've got no doubt they cared about each other," I said.

"That's an interesting response." Detective Jones rubbed his mustache for a second time, taking longer than the first time. "Tommy's parents and sister paint a different picture."

"You've spoken to them?" I asked.

"Yes, we have," Detective Jones said.

"I'm sorry to disappoint you, but if there's something juicy to know, then I'm not the one to tell you," I said.

"No shit," Detective Garrison said.

Perhaps Detective Garrison should've seen a proctologist. There was no reason for his current demeanor. It wasn't like I did anything to him.

I might not have been a detective, but that wasn't required for agreeing with Detective Jones. If Detective Garrison and Jones—or any other cop—expected civilian cooperation, then they needed to present themselves in a warm light. Instead, either one of them could have been cast as the witch from Hansel and Gretel.

Detective Jones patted my shoulder. "Don't fret, dear. You did a great job, and we appreciate your cooperation."

"Speak for yourself," Detective Garrison touted.

"We'll let ourselves out." Detective Jones dragged her partner by the arm and the door slammed behind them after a beat.

I pressed my hand against my neck once their car's clunky ignition was no longer audible. Catching my breath was the least I deserved. Panic was still mandatory, even if I wasn't a suspect. If Mallory was a person of interest, then that could unravel everything from the night of the Snowflake Ball, and I might've been headed to prison.

So, maybe, just maybe, Gemma's offer screamed at me more and more with each passing second. If Mallory was gonna go down for killing Tommy, then she might as well have gone down in a way that didn't expose Archie and me. It was something to think about. I didn't have unlimited chances and had to give Gemma an answer at some point.

FRIDAY, JANUARY 18, 2019

I walked down the hallway on my way to my locker before first period, only for my heart to flutter.

Mallory stood by Archie's locker, yet it wasn't their conversation that concerned me. Mallory's posture would cause me to need Botox for the frown lines currently creasing my face. Her hands were around Archie's neck, straightening the collar of his polo shirt.

"What's going on here?" I asked a moment later.

Mallory laughed. "Nothing. Your boyfriend is a slob, and I was just doing him a favor."

"There was nothing wrong with my collar," Archie said.

"It was crooked, and your buttons were undone," Mallory said.

Archie gawked at her. "I didn't realize you worked for the fashion police."

"Chad deserves a decent boyfriend," Mallory said.

Deep breaths. They were only laughing—it wasn't like I walked in on them in bed.

I might not have had to find them having sex for almost screaming, though. Flirting with Archie in front of me was the ultimate treachery. If I said anything, then I'd resemble someone who needed counseling. Being labeled a lunatic was the last thing I needed when I had my whole life ahead of me.

"Something wrong?" Mallory asked.

"I just miss winter break," I said. "We're lucky that we have two weeks off as opposed to all the other neighboring towns."

Archie clapped my shoulder. "Tell me about it. Nothing like waking up past noon."

"Are you sure everything is okay?" Mallory asked, raising her voice slightly. "You don't seem fine, and we'd want to know if something was wrong."

Wait. She might've been trying to provoke me, and I couldn't have that. I wouldn't lose my relationship with Archie on an impulsive whim.

My smile expanded. "Yeah. Everything is fine."

What Archie didn't know wouldn't hurt him. No big deal if this conversation made me closer to accepting Gemma's offer. I'd do whatever action necessary to save my relationship with Archie. Nothing would stop me.

MONDAY, JANUARY 21, 2019

I sat in Kelly's office, sipping tea during one of my free periods.

Chatting with Kelly somehow seemed like a good idea—even if being Mallory's sister meant having some innate sense of loyalty despite their mutual hatred. Talking to a stranger was sometimes easier than talking to a friend or family member.

"Thank you for meeting with me even though it's not about a school matter," I said.

She raised her palms at me. "Please. I'm always happy to meet with students."

"You might wanna lock your door for this one."

"Okay." Kelly rose, then shuffled towards the door. It clinked after another beat before she returned to her chair. "What's up?"

"What if you had to do something terrible?" I asked.

Her elbows slid onto her desk. "I have no problem talking, but we need to get a few things straight."

"Excuse me?"

"If you're thinking about hurting yourself, then I'd have to report it."

Kelly needed a dose of reality ASAP. I wasn't sure how she could make the leap to suicide. That was a big stretch even if teachers and adults had to be more sensitive about students' emotional needs.

"This has nothing to do with depression or suicide," I said.

"You sure?" she asked.

Okay. Either Kelly cared about her job or she was really neurotic. I hadn't given Kelly any indication about intending to harm myself, because that possibility wasn't an option. Not now, not ever. I had too much to live for—whether it was my writing, Archie, or post high school life. And Kelly would drop the inquisition if she knew what was best for her. Further questions about my mental health would've only wasted time.

"Yes." I took a bigger sip of my tea this time. "Actually, it's about someone you know."

"Don't tell me it's about the Tommy situation? I thought we agreed to keep our mouths shut and keep things vague with the police?"

"This isn't about the Tommy situation," I lied.

Her eyes practically bugged out of her head. "It's not?"

"Nope. But I'm not at liberty to say more."

"I can do vague."

"Someone made me an offer and I'm not sure if I should accept or not," I said.

She finished the rest of her tea. "You might have to be a little more specific."

"It's better if I'm not."

"You're scaring me."

Please. No need for Kelly's fake concern. Not after some of the things I knew about her. She'd done much worse and shouldn't've waited till now to develop a conscience.

"This deal would secure my future." I gulped my tea. "Although someone would get hurt, and I'm not sure if I could live with that."

"I've got a question for you," Kelly said.

"I'm listening."

She drummed her fingers against her desk. "Does the person deserve it?"

The events of the last few months flashed through my mind. More specifically, Mallory's menacing look when I talked to Archie the first time, her indecent proposal, the detectives being onto Mallory anyway, and Mallory getting cute with Archie. And there're more things Mallory might've done that escaped me for the moment.

I didn't even blink. "Yes. This person is the worst."

"Then you've got your answer."

TUESDAY, JANUARY 22, 2019

I sat down in one of the leather lounge chairs at Café Tomorrow after school.

"About time." Gemma closed her book, then shoved it to the side. "I'm not a patient person and need an answer."

I hesitated. "I've never done this type of thing before."

"I understand, but that's not an answer."

I cleared my throat. "I'll help you on one condition."

Gemma pushed her headband further up her head. "And what's that?"

"Nobody can ever know about this arrangement."

"Fine by me. Now how about we get some beverages and discuss what we should do?"

"Great. I'd like a large, hot caramel macchiato—your treat."

"Fair enough." Gemma rose, then got in line while my stomach sank.

I had to keep reminding myself I was doing what needed to be done.

I could accept my behavior someday—that was just wasn't today. Not when Mallory's face remained burned in my mind. Her hyena facial expression from when she spied on my first conversation with Archie was nothing compared to the look Mallory would give when she discovered I was responsible for her downfall.

BEFORE

TUESDAY, OCTOBER 16, 2018

Not having concrete proof of Mallory's involvement with Tommy's disappearance didn't stop me from doing something about my suspicions. Being wrong was the worst thing that could happen. Besides, I needed to protect myself. As much as I might've prided myself with not being vengeful like Mallory—such as with her dating Archie to hurt me—information might still be useful.

So, yeah. I sat on Tommy and Gemma's living room couch after school. Yet I wasn't there to see Gemma.

Mrs. Drake smiled at me. "It's good to see you, dear. I can't tell you how disappointed I was when Tommy ditched you freshman year."

I shifted my weight. "Don't worry about it. There's nothing you can do now."

"Doesn't mean I'm happy with him."

"Gemma had the same reaction," I said.

"I don't blame her." She paused for a second, clutching her pearl necklace. "Nor do I blame myself. My unconditional love doesn't mean I agree with everything Tommy did."

"If only more parents were as realistic as you."

Mrs. Drake grabbed her mug on the mahogany table in front of us, then sipped her tea. "What can I do for you?"

"This subject might be difficult for you, but I don't have a choice."

She beamed her eyes. "Let me guess. You wanna discuss Tommy?"

Creepy. First Gemma read my mind and now Mrs. Drake.

Deep breaths. It wasn't like someone implanted a chip in my brain and all my thoughts were visible to the public. I just should've been less obvious about my thoughts and feelings.

"I'm not trying to offend you," I said.

"Stop. You never have to apologize for anything." She snatched a cookie from the tin next to her cup, then made a series of crunching noises.

Funny. I wouldn't have expected someone who wore a pearl necklace, cardigan, Gucci blouse and matching pants, with hair wrapped in a bun to be so blasé about proper etiquette.

Or maybe I just didn't wanna believe Mallory was as evil as that day at Café Tomorrow when she confessed to pursuing Archie out of spite and didn't want to know if she was behind what happened to Tommy. Whether logical or not, people were full of contradictions. Like someone who didn't drink but was a chain smoker, or someone that had high blood pressure yet low sodium.

Mrs. Drake cracked her knuckles. "Just say whatever you wanna say. I promise I won't get angry."

Implicating Mallory in whatever happened to Tommy might've added more drama to the situation, yet I could talk around the issue.

"What was your opinion of Mallory?" I asked.

Her gaze narrowed. "Why do you ask?"

I shrugged. "Let's just say my opinion of Mallory has changed."

"Do you know something?"

"Gemma just mentioned how Tommy isolated himself for Mallory. Tell me something. Do you agree with her assessment?"

"Yes," Mrs. Drake said, nodding. "That girl is poison."

Interesting. Good to know Gemma and I weren't the only ones with a negative opinion of Mallory—so my feelings couldn't have been in my head.

"I also know about the missing money," I said.

Mrs. Drake snorted. "Gemma has a big mouth."

"I never said Gemma told me."

"You didn't have to." Mrs. Drake reached for her tea, then finished the rest of it. She even belched.

"What do you think happened to Tommy?" I asked.

"He probably raided his trust fund and ran away—he's always been a rebellious kid." Mrs. Drake inhaled a breath. "It wasn't like there were any age restrictions on it. He's always had access to it—like an allowance in one lump sum."

Mrs. Drake peeked at her watch, then her shoulders tensed. "I should get dinner started—Marcus doesn't like it when dinner is late."

At the mention of her husband, I couldn't stop myself from chuckling. Even I wouldn't have worried about something as frivolous as dinner being a couple minutes behind schedule. There were more serious issues worth contemplating. And if Mr. Drake had that type of reaction over something insignificant, then I wouldn't have wanted to be around him when something serious happened.

"It's only a little before four," I said.

"Doesn't matter. The pot roast will take a while. Chatting with you was nice, though."

"Same." I rose, then froze. I didn't know how I first missed the issue, but Mrs. Drake's left wrist was black and blue. "What happened to your hand?"

"I'm just clumsy."

"Yeah, I know the feeling." I was almost out of the living room when Mrs. Drake hollered at me.

"Yes?" I asked.

"I should apologize to you."

I blinked. "Excuse me?"

"I shouldn't have let Tommy cut you out of his life," Mrs. Drake said. "Although I've got my own theories about why he did that."

"I'm not following."

"He was just so fond of you—always talking about you in the afternoons when he came home from school." Mrs. Drake gripped her pearl necklace even tighter this time. In fact, the necklace would've broken if her hold increased anymore. "Like when I first dated Marcus in my junior year of high school."

No way. She couldn't have just implied Tommy had a crush on me—even if there was more stuff with Tommy that I hadn't unpacked. That was like saying someone had a 99 percent chance of being the victim of an alien abduction.

"You really should leave—you don't need to be here when Marcus arrives," Mrs. Drake said.

"Sure. Thanks again." I darted out of the living room, shuffling towards the front door.

The door burst open, and a man glared at me. "Long time no see, Chad."

"Mr. Drake," I mumbled.

"What are you doing here?" Mr. Drake stepped inside, then placed his briefcase on the table by the door.

"I was reminiscing with Mrs. Drake about Tommy," I said.

"Call me Lisa," Mrs. Drake chirped.

Mr. Drake scowled. "Mrs. Drake is fine. It's important for children to know their place in the world."

"Absolutely," I said.

Mr. Drake rolled up his sleeves. "What did you guys discuss about Tommy?"

"Nothing important," I interrupted.

"I'll be the judge of that," Mr. Drake said.

"He wanted to know my theories about Tommy," Mrs. Drake said.

Mr. Drake cackled. "No need to chat with my wife. I could've given you the truth."

If I didn't know better, then I would've accused Mr. Drake of being sexist. This wasn't the 1800's, and he didn't need to speak for his wife.

Sweat dripped down my back. "Oh, yeah? And what's that?"

"The ungrateful shit is probably sitting on a beach somewhere, pissing away his trust fund."

Ouch. Even if Mr. Drake didn't approve of Tommy's choices, he still shouldn't have referred to his son like that—as if he didn't care if the police found Tommy.

"Anyway, I should get going," I said.

Mr. Drake craned his neck. "Sure thing. But you've got an open invitation to stop by whenever you want."

"Thanks." The front door clinked behind me, and I stood on the front porch for a beat.

Yup. Goosebumps covered my arms and legs even though I couldn't be sure of what happened in Gemma's house behind closed doors. If Mr. Drake wanted people to have a good impression of him, then he hadn't done himself any favors. At a first glance, Mrs. Drake's "clumsy" explanation proved innocent yet—combined with Mr. Drake's sexism— I wondered if something more sinister was happening in their house.

What exactly my curiosity entailed was a question for another day. Just like the Mallory situation, I didn't have much to hold onto. But I couldn't say I was surprised—it was just like the universe. Expecting to find answers about one thing, only for the conversation to take another turn.

So, there was only one thing for me to do—continue digging till I uncovered the truth.

WEDNESDAY, OCTOBER 17, 2018

Sunlight radiated from the sky while Archie and I stood on the tennis court of the local country club, which we had to ourselves.

I put my hands in front of my eyes, studying the opposite end of the tennis court. "You should be proud of yourself. You're the only person who has ever gotten me to play sports."

"First time for everything," Archie said.

"You're probably gonna win—my aim is off."

"Let me help you." Archie walked to my side of the court, then took out an extra tennis ball from his pocket. He placed the tennis ball in my hand before standing behind me. After that, Archie wrapped his arms around mine, guiding them until smacking the tennis ball to the left of where Archie stood moments earlier.

I laughed. "Not bad."

"Maybe I should've suggested something else for our date."

"I wanna be interested in things you like."

"Our relationship will survive if we don't like the same things."

I sighed. "I know. But I don't wanna be a buzzkill."

"You aren't if you're being your true self. I'm also secure enough in our relationship not to freak out over a small thing."

Relationship. There that word was again—Archie mentioned it twice in a short amount of time.

So, yeah. I stroked my chin. Just because we got a chance, didn't mean I labeled our interactions. Even if I wanted to be more than friends with him. Doing so too soon would've scared him away, and I would've kicked myself if that happened. The universe was bound to disappoint me again, so I'd enjoy happiness while I could.

He raised his eyebrows. "What's wrong?"

"Nothing."

"You're thinking about something."

"It's nice you referred to our dynamic as a relationship."

Archie winked. "What should I have referred to this as?"

"No. Relationship was the right word."

Archie looped his arms around my neck, then stared into my eyes. "Glad we're on the same page. Anyway, would you wanna grab some frozen yogurt?"

"Sure. I'll spoil my dinner for you."

"Good to know I'm special." He pressed his lips against mine before placing his hands on my cheeks.

Regardless of the truth about Mallory and Mr. Drake, I appreciated the simplicity of this moment with Archie. And not because it'd be fleeting like everything else in life. Archie and I were able to have a conversation about our dynamic without arguing. And said fact was worth everything in the world. Sometimes, one wrong turn in a conversation ended a relationship before it blossomed into its full, epic potential.

THURSDAY, OCTOBER 18, 2018

I arrived home from school, only to be greeted by the warm aroma of apples, sugar, and cinnamon while Mom stood in front of the oven, sipping coffee.

"Hi, honey," she said.

"Don't tell me something bad happened?"

She gave me a dirty look. "I don't need a reason to bake. Can't I just do something nice?"

"If you insist." I shuffled to the fridge and grabbed a diet ginger ale.

"You seem extra happy." Mom placed her mug on the kitchen counter next to the oven. "Does it have anything to do with Archie."

"That obvious?"

"There's no shame in being happy. Archie is your first real relationship."

"Don't have to tell me that."

"Does he treat you right?" Mom asked.

"Yeah, I'm a lucky guy."

"Just don't move too fast."

I almost choked on my soda. "Come again?"

"There's plenty of time for you to have adult experiences."

Mom couldn't have implied what I suspected. I'd rather experience nails across a chalkboard than have this conversation. Not every cliché teen experience had to come. I'd be fine if Mom didn't discuss "the birds and the bees."

I folded my arms. "You aren't trying to have a sex talk with me, are you?"

"I'm your mother."

Please. As if that gave her a right to discuss something so personal—I never once asked her any nosey questions.

"That doesn't have mean I wanna discuss this with you. Have you heard of the internet?" I asked.

"Please be careful," Mom said.

"Sex is probably the last thing on Archie's mind."

"Don't sell yourself short. Anyone would be lucky to have you."

If a serial killer from a 1980's slasher moved appeared in my kitchen and slit my throat, I wouldn't have complained. Disbelief flooded my body since a couple minutes into this conversation. My potential sex life shouldn't have resembled a seventh grader dissecting a frog in Biology. Some things—like whether I'd get naked with another human being—were meant to stay private.

"You're my mother—you've gotta have a positive opinion of me," I said.

The oven chimed.

"Maybe." Mom slid the oven mitts onto her hands, then opened the oven, allowing the heat from it to permeate the kitchen. "But that doesn't mean I'm wrong."

"Whatever you say."

"I'm surprised about one thing, though." Mom placed the tray containing the pie on the middle of the stove. Then, she tossed the oven mitts aside. "I always thought you'd end up with Tommy."

Mom and Mrs. Drake must've been drinking the same the Kool-Aid. Not once had I ever looked at Tommy as more than a friend—even in light of that incident between us that I still wasn't ready to address. Not because he was ugly, but because boundaries were sometimes important. Like with how I didn't wanna be more than friends with Mallory. Her not being terrible to look at didn't mean we had to indulge our teenage hormones.

"How so?" I asked.

"You two used to be so close in middle school. Whatever. Dynamics change, and your current happiness is the only thing that matters."

FRIDAY, OCTOBER 19, 2018

I strutted through the school hallway before first period, only to shake my head.

Mallory stood by Archie's locker, but them being together wasn't why my stomach remained tangled. Mallory's gesticulating and her constipated facial expression was why someone needed to call the UN.

"What's going on?" I asked.

"We were arguing about whether or not it would rain tomorrow," Mallory said.

I turned to Archie. "Is she telling the truth?"

"Yes," Archie said.

Mallory licked her lips. "I'll give you two a moment, but this isn't over, Archie. I'll prove to you that it's gonna rain tomorrow if it's the last thing I do."

Mallory and Archie couldn't have been arguing about the weather. And my reasoning wasn't about being cynical. The weather was what people discussed when they didn't actually want to chat about the real problem. Although I wasn't sure if I could handle discovering what they talked about before my arrival—I couldn't unlearn something once I learned it. Knowing Mallory, the topic of conversation must've been something bad. Even if I "forgave" Mallory, I couldn't forget her using

Archie as a pawn. Archie hadn't deserved that. Mallory's problem was with me, not him.

"Give it your best shot," Archie touted.

Mallory darted down the hallway and was soon out of sight.

I glanced back at Archie. "Tell me the truth? Were you really arguing about the weather?"

"Why is that so hard to believe?" Archie asked.

"Have you forgotten everything Mallory has done?"

Archie wrapped around his hands around my neck, pulling me up against his body. After that, he resumed his soulful gaze. "Stop worrying."

"I appreciate you not retaliating against Mallory because of her pursuing you to hurt me. However, you don't have to be positive all the time."

"I'm not lying."

I rolled my eyes. "Whatever you say. But don't say I didn't give you an opportunity to be honest."

"There's something else we should discuss," Archie said.

"And what's that?"

He bit his lip. "We haven't had the talk yet."

Perhaps Mom was psychic. Archie and I couldn't have been about to have the sex conversation, yet here I was, stomach in my throat. No amount of time we spent together changed how I never considered what my first time would be like.

"Great. Bring it on," I said.

He quirked his eyebrows. "What? Have you never been with someone before?"

Yeah. I should've played poker. At least then I would've known how to hide my feelings more. Just because I had a feeling or opinion didn't mean the whole world needed to know about it.

"It's nothing to be embarrassed about," Archie continued.

"Easy for you to say. I'm sure you've been with hundreds of people."

Archie glared at me.

"I was kidding," I said.

"I know. I was giving you a hard time."

"I don't even know where to begin," I said.

"I have a few ideas."

One. Two. Three. Four. Five. Six. Seven. Eight. Nine. Ten. Life would be okay. Regardless of my cheeks being redder than Santa Claus's suit, this conversation might not have been entirely unexpected. That day at the tennis court electrified every neuron in my body. My blood couldn't help pumping through my veins faster with Archie leaning against me. Almost as if that day was the opening act to sleeping with Archie for the first time.

SUNDAY, OCTOBER 21, 2018

Archie locked the door while I stood in front of my bed.

"Are we really doing this?" I asked.

"We can wait if you want to. You never get your first time back."

Once again, even the simplest statements contained the most profound truth. No matter how much I wished I had a time machine and could undo something if it didn't go well, life didn't work that way. Sometimes, people just lived with the disappointment no matter how much the pain ached.

Archie smiled. "Well?"

"I've never been surer of anything in my life." I pulled Archie in for a kiss.

What happened next compared to a movie montage, because time didn't freeze no matter how appealing the idea was. And a trail of our clothes soon littered my bedroom floor while Archie leaned against me.

"I love you so much," Archie said.

I cocked my head, hands still wrapped in Archie's. "Me too."

He pressed his lips against mine, their soft texture caressing my mouth. We might not have had forever, but we had right now. And that was enough.

AFTER

FRIDAY, FEBRUARY 1, 2019

I sat at an empty cafeteria table before first period, finishing homework from my Algebra 2 class. Apparently, some things escaped me no matter how diligent I was—I could've sworn I did the assignment last night.

Someone tapped my back.

I lifted my gaze off my textbook and notebook. "Excited for the weekend, Mallory?"

"Yeah." She twisted a strand of hair around her finger. "Mind if I sit?"

The constricted feeling returned to my throat.

Being at school didn't mean I forgot about my scheming with Gemma—I hadn't. So, a conversation might give me guilt pangs. Yet I couldn't do anything to Mallory. Tipping her off was the last thing I needed. Gemma was probably more dangerous than Mallory—her hatred for Mallory was palpable. If I hadn't agreed to help Gemma, then she might've resorted to violence for punishing Mallory. In a way, I looked out for Mallory. Even if Mallory would never see it that way if she discovered the truth.

"Well?" Mallory asked.

I nodded. "Sure. Company would be nice."

"Thanks." Mallory shifted her posture after sitting down next to me. "Anyway, I owe you an apology."

"For what?"

"That day in the hallway when I chatted with Archie. I didn't realize it at first, but it looked bad."

Shit. Mallory's contrition didn't help me. If anything, I would've been able to sleep better at night if she did something even worse than her indecent proposal. At least then I wouldn't have had any doubts about working with Gemma.

"Don't worry about it." I scribbled the question's answer down in my notebook. "You can talk with Archie as much as you want."

"That's kind of you to say, but please don't make excuses for me. My therapist says honesty is the only way for me be emotionally healthy."

"You like your counselor?"

"Yes, I do. He's neither condescending nor too blunt."

"As long as it helps."

"It is—I'm gonna have a great life, and there's nothing that bitch Gemma Drake can do about it."

Gemma. If a conversation or event didn't return to Mallory, it came back to Gemma. I didn't have my head stuck up my ass, and I'd have to tell her how I'd get the proof she needed to destroy Mallory—like how Kelly stored the flash drive and Tommy's gun.

"Are you sure you're okay?" Mallory asked.

"Just school stress."

She patted my hand. "You'll be fine."

Wait. Not gloating to Mallory about my intentions with Gemma's didn't mean I couldn't alleviate some guilt. Like with how Detective Garrison and Jones tried getting information from me. The revelation might even make Mallory trust me more, which might help my scheming with Gemma.

"I haven't been honest with you," I said.

She giggled. "Don't tell me you and Gemma are secretly best friends?"

Creepy. Her joke shouldn't have been closer to the truth than she realized. There was good intuition and then there was the freaky kind of sixth sense.

"I didn't wanna alarm you, but the detectives assigned to Tommy's case recently chatted with me," I said. "I just said I didn't know anything apart from how you and Tommy seemed content. Although I emphasized your relationship must've had its challenges like any other couple so they wouldn't be too suspicious."

"Perfect," she said.

"I should've told you sooner."

"Don't worry about it. The detectives also spoke to me, but I basically said the same thing you did."

"Great minds think alike."

"No shit." Mallory remained silent for as second. "Please don't feel like you have to hide things from me. If we're gonna survive the Tommy situation, then we need to be honest with each other."

"Thanks for not getting angry." I jotted down an answer in my notebook after solving another problem.

"I could never be annoyed with you—we're in this together."

"When's your next counseling appointment?" I asked.

"Next Tuesday after school. Although Kelly is instant on driving me—something about wanting to be more supportive."

What Mallory didn't know was I needed to find the perfect time to break into Kelly's safe. So, yeah. I was going to Hell. The only question was how soon it'd happen.

I feigned a smile. "Hope it goes well."

TUESDAY, FEBRUARY 5, 2019

"Are you sure you wanna do this?" I asked.

Gemma and I stood by Kelly and Mallory's front door, yet I almost hoped Gemma changed her mind. It wasn't too late to abandon our mission. Nobody knew what we were up to, and we could pretend we never concocted this revenge plot. No matter how jealousy of Mallory flared through my body, I couldn't undo our plan once we did it.

She snorted. "Don't be ridiculous. It's bad enough that you stalled again after agreeing to help me. So, we're doing this."

"Okay. Whatever you say."

"Imagine how good it'll feel once we decimate Mallory."

I leaned down, then got the spare key under the doormat. The lock's sharp click echoed, and we entered the home.

"Do you know how to break into a safe?" Gemma asked a couple of minutes later.

We currently stood in Kelly's bedroom by her dresser, which the metal safe rested on.

I was about ready to give Gemma a dirty look, though. She should've had more faith in me—I wouldn't have suggested this if I didn't know what I was doing.

"Yes," I touted. "Mallory and I have broken into the safe a once or twice over the last couple years, and I saw Mallory do the combination."

Gemma let out a breath. "Okay. Cool."

"We can't be too careful." I grabbed the latex gloves from my beach bag, then put them on. "We don't wanna implicate ourselves."

She grinned. "You're genius. I would've never thought about fingertips."

I did the combination, then Gemma cackled.

"What's the problem now?" I asked. "I'm doing exactly what you wanted. I mean, would some gratitude kill you?"

"I just find it funny how the combination is 6-6-6."

Perhaps Gemma already spent too much time with me. Getting distracted over something like the safe's combination was something I would've done. If she was really so concerned about her mission, then she should've been more focused.

The safe remained open while we continued standing in front of it.

"Don't just stand there—do something," Gemma said.

"We're taking the gun and flash drive. And we should steal Mallory's diary from her bedroom."

"Why do we need Mallory's diary?"

"She wrote about her hatred for you in it—like discovering you and Tommy in bed together."

Gemma grimaced. "I'm not sure if I wanna do this. What if I get in trouble for my affair with Tommy?"

Please. Gemma needed a good look in the mirror. She couldn't have waited till now for realizing her relationship with Tommy might be exposed. Even a five-year-old could've figured out that point.

"He's dead," I blurted.

She shook her head. "You're right."

I waved the items at her. "I'm holding onto the gun, flash drive, and diary until we decide what we're gonna do with them."

"I can live with that."

Phew. Gemma was smart for once in her life. Arguing about who held onto the evidence would've only caused problems we didn't need. If we were gonna work together, then we couldn't bicker.

I almost closed the safe when a manila envelope stuffed in back behind a couple necklaces caught my attention. So, I did what I always did—I inserted myself into a situation that might not have been any of my business.

"What are you doing?" Gemma asked.

"One second." I peeked inside the manila envelope after grabbing it. There were two newspaper clippings inside, and I slid them out. Both articles were of local boys in our grade who died within the last couple years. The first guy was Parker—he was Mallory's boyfriend before Tommy and also cheated on her. The other was Jordon—he was the boyfriend of one Mallory's friends from the debate and cheated on his girlfriend like Parker had on Mallory. My jaw shook after another beat.

They both died of drownings—Parker in his pool whereas Jordon died in his hot tub.

Wait. Jordon and Parker didn't only have something in common with each other—they also shared a similarity with Tommy. Cheating.

Gemma whimpered. "What's wrong?"

"See for yourself." I handed Gemma the articles.

She gasped. "Are you implying what I think you are?"

"I don't know. Tell me what you're thinking."

"We found these in Kelly's safe."

"Yeah."

"And I can only think of one reason why Kelly would have these—she was suspicious of Mallory."

"Mallory is a lot of things, but she's not a murderer," I said.

Someone should've given me a Nobel Peace Prize—I still defended Mallory in light of everything she had done to me. Doing so was something most people wouldn't have done. A part of me yearned for simpler times—like in middle school before Tommy ditched me for the cool kids.

"It's kind of convenient how they were both cheaters and drowned," Gemma said.

"Almost as if lightning struck twice."

"Even more reason to take down Mallory—she's a serial killer."

My shoulders quaked. "We don't know that."

"Quit making excuses—you agreed to help me."

"We should go get Mallory's diary before her and Kelly come home," I said.

"Agreed."

I put the newspaper clippings back in the envelope before tucking it inside the safe by the jewelry. After that, I closed the safe.

We shuffled out of Kelly's bedroom before darting towards Mallory's and grabbing her diary.

Except we didn't count on footsteps when we were ready to leave Mallory's bedroom.

Gemma and I looked at each other.

"Bummer about the counseling appoint ending early," Mallory bellowed. "But let me change my sweater and then we can go for pizza."

The footsteps grew louder and louder with each passing second.

Shit. We only had a matter of seconds before Mallory caught us.

I threw a gaze towards the closet door, and Gemma nodded. Then, we rushed into the closet, making sure not to slam the door. No point in hiding if Mallory would discover us.

The footsteps stopped.

"Never mind," Mallory said, voice echoing. "My current sweater is warm enough."

The footsteps once again echoed, but this time they grew faint and fainter until they were no longer audible. Gemma and I exchanged a second glance after another beat. My pulse stopped soaring while I caught my breath.

Thank goodness the universe wasn't in the mood to screw me over this afternoon. I didn't know what I would've done if Mallory discovered us.

WEDNESDAY, FEBRUARY 6, 2019

"Thanks for coming with me," Dan said.

I snickered. "No problem."

"I couldn't do this by myself."

"No explanation necessary. There's no point in having a bisexual best friend if I can't give you fashion advice."

Dan and I stood by a clothing rack at Angelica's—a women's clothing shop at the local mall.

"Although I can't believe Rebecca trusted you with her sizes," I continued.

"We've been dating since the seventh grade."

"Don't have to tell me that."

He wiped a bead of sweat from his forehead. "I'm serious about appreciating your presence, because I'm gonna buy you dinner after this."

"That isn't necessary."

"It's not like I have anything better to do—Rebecca is busy studying for her French test."

I elbowed him. "Fantastic. Glad I'm your priority."

"Don't make it sound worse than it is."

I handed Dan a hot-pink colored dress. "Get this. Rebecca has always danced around a gutsy wardrobe but hasn't had the confidence to embrace a bolder style."

"Let's see how much the dress costs first." Dan surveyed the price tag. "Wow. A lot less than I expected."

"Perfect."

"How are things with you and Archie?" Dan asked.

Interesting. I hadn't expected the conversation to change topics. As much as I might've cared about Archie, teaming up with Gemma still lurked in the back of my mind—Gemma wasn't that far of a leap from Archie, because my whole alliance with her was about protecting my relationship with Archie. And the Gemma situation would probably be on my mind for some time—we still had to figure out how to plant the evidence on Mallory.

"They're fine," I said.

He frowned. "You're no longer worried about Mallory?"

"Nah. Some things look worse than they are."

"Wow." Dan rubbed my shoulder. "I'm proud of you."

"Jealousy was a wasted emotion."

His stomach grumbled. "Let's hurry up and go pay for this dress, because I don't know how much longer I can wait till dinner."

"Sounds good."

THURSDAY, FEBRUARY 7, 2019

I closed my locker after getting everything I needed for my morning, then Kelly grabbed my arm. "My office now," she said.

Yikes. Both the inflection and tone in her voice comforted me. NOT. I so wanted to be accosted by someone before my day began.

"What's this about?" I asked.

"Not here."

Kelly continued dragging me until we reached her office. She tossed me inside before locking the door.

"Do you wanna tell me what's going on?" I spat.

"I know about everything."

"I don't know what you're referring to."

Yeah. Even if I deduced what she was getting at, I still wouldn't show my hand. Information was power, and I wouldn't give Kelly any leverage. Not when one thing could ruin everything Gemma and I planned.

Kelly wove her arms together. "Cut the bullshit. It's only you and me."

"You're gonna have to be more specific."

"The gun and flash drive are missing from my safe and Mallory is pissed she can't find her diary," Kelly revealed.

Ouch. Any hope for Kelly not knowing what was happening vanished, and I'd scream at the universe later. It wouldn't have been the end of the world if one thing went right for me—that was the least I deserved.

"What does that have to do with me?" I asked.

"I remember our conversation from the other day," Kelly said. "The one about needing help making a decision."

Wow. Good for Kelly. She could be a police consultant if she wanted, because her determination was the type of behavior needed for solving cases. And said fact was so lovely. I cherished every complication that happened in my life.

I clamped my lips together. "You're gonna have to be more specific."

"You wanna frame Mallory for killing Tommy—don't you?"

"It's not staging anything if Mallory is guilty."

"How can you do this to your best friend?" Kelly asked.

"I'm never gonna be able to trust her. She used my relationship with Archie to hurt me, and I can't take that risk. Not anymore."

"Do you realize how insecure you sound?"

Kelly shouldn't have judged me. Nobody was perfect—including her—so I'd be damned if I let her judge me. Not when I had more important issues to focus on. Like how Gemma and I would set up Mallory without making the police interested in us.

"I don't have a choice," I said.

The vein on her forehead surfaced. "Jealousy doesn't excuse your actions. Mallory is going to therapy and trying to find healthy coping mechanisms for her grief."

"I know about her counseling. How do you think I found the time to break into her home?" I asked.

Kelly rubbed her lip. "Wait? Were you in the house on Tuesday when Mallory and I arrived home early from her appointment?"

"Yeah. I was."

"Wait till Mallory finds out the truth." Kelly reached for her iPhone, but I snatched it off her desk before she could grab it.

Using force might not have made me all warm and fuzzy, yet I didn't wanna harm Kelly. She just needed to know I was not someone to be messed with. Besides, I couldn't forget her getting physical with me when she confronted me by my locker moments earlier. So, in a way, she brought this escalation on herself.

"You aren't gonna snitch on me," I said.

"And why is that?" Kelly asked.

"I know things about you—things that would end you."

"I don't give into threats."

"It's not a threat. But go ahead and try me—I dare you."

Kelly cringed. "Are you talking about what I think you are?"

I shrugged. "I don't know—what do you think I'm getting at? You've done a lot of nasty stuff over the years."

Yup. Knowledge was still power, and I wouldn't reveal my information. Not when this nugget might help me at some point in the future. So, Kelly could beg all she wanted, yet I wouldn't budge.

She made a fist. "Fine. I won't say anything to Mallory. But you're still a terrible friend to her."

Please. More than tough talk was required for me to flinch—Mallory had said much worse to me, and I'd be fine.

"You're also a hypocrite," I said.

"You've already threatened me."

"This isn't about you."

"Then what?" Kelly barked.

"It was the newspaper clippings inside the envelope."

She grunted. "Saving old newspaper articles isn't a crime."

"But murder is."

"Excuse me?" Kelly asked, almost choking on a breath.

I towered over her, standing on my tip toes. "There's only one reason you'd save those articles and it's not because your nostalgic."

"I don't like being told what to think."

Gemma and Mallory might not have been the only ones who needed counseling. If Kelly couldn't deal with her feelings—like knowing Mallory killed before, then she might've also benefited from professional help.

"Do you really think Mallory killed Parker and Jordon?" I asked.

"Leave. I've got nothing else to say to you."

"Fine. Have a great day." I unlocked her door, then dashed down the hallway.

I turned the corner, and a faint smile tugged at my lips. Archie was a few feet away from me, and that was exactly what I needed. Even spending a few minutes with him reminded me of what I was fighting for.

BEFORE

TUESDAY, OCTOBER 23, 2018

Archie and I sat at one of the tables in front of the high school's main entrance during lunch. There wasn't one cloud in the sky, and we needed to enjoy the sunshine before the typical fall chill permeated the New England air.

Just because it wasn't cold or raining didn't mean lunch would be picturesque, though. Mallory just exited the door, heading towards us.

Archie winced. "There's something I've gotta tell you, Chad. But you aren't gonna like this."

I squeezed his hand. "You can tell me anything. I'd rather you be honest than lie."

Encouraging honesty didn't make me naïve—I didn't expect Archie to confess every misdeed in his life. But if he did something to hurt me—whether physically or emotionally—I'd rather him tell me then someone else.

Mallory grinned. "Hi, guys."

"I don't mean to be rude but we're in the middle of a conversation," I said.

Mallory flipped her hair over her shoulders. "Save me the fake sincerity. You don't care about being rude."

"You're right; I don't," I said.

Archie's jaw shuddered. "I was about to tell him something important."

"Too late—I'm bored," Mallory said.

I glared at her. "I don't understand what you're getting at."

"It's simple," Mallory said. "I discovered Archie's father lost his job, but his mother doesn't know yet."

"Get to the point," I spat.

Archie gritted his teeth. "Mallory, please!"

Shit. I didn't need a high school diploma for deducing this conversation would probably take an unpleasant turn. So, I could only hope the destruction wouldn't be too bad. Just because the universe might've been out to get me didn't mean the damage had to be the worst every time something bad happened to me.

"You had your chance, but it's too late," Mallory said.

"All you're doing is ruining my lunch." I snapped my can of diet ginger ale open, then took a big sip. "Just go."

"Your day is going to get worse," Mallory said.

Good graciousness. So much for embracing optimism for one fleeting moment. The glee radiating from Mallory's face provided the most important clue about the conversation's direction. She was having way too much fun, and I couldn't wait to figure out what twisted scheme she cooked up this time.

Archie gave Mallory a look. "You don't have to do this. You already hurt Chad when you went out with me."

"Remember how Archie reunited with you unexpectedly?" Mallory asked.

"Yes. But what does that have to do with anything?" I demanded.

Her smile expanded. "I blackmailed Archie to get back together with you and then dump you after sleeping with you."

"What?" I stammered.

"I thought you deserved to know the truth," Mallory said.

Archie grumbled. "Don't pretend you're doing Chad any favors."

No shit. Even a five-year-old could've deduced this conversation wouldn't have been better for Mallory if she gotten into her first-choice college.

"Say what you want about me, but Archie agreeing to this indecent proposal says more about him than me," Mallory said.

I rubbed my lower lip. "Wait? Is that why you two argued the other day?"

"Yes," Archie said. "I changed my mind and Mallory wasn't having it."

"Why not tell Archie's mother the truth then?" I asked.

"This does more damage," Mallory said.

Great. Any hope of Mallory and I becoming friends again vanished. Getting revenge was one thing—everyone was human and made mistakes—yet causing the most hurt possible revealed a crueler person than I could've ever imagined.

"I only did it to protect my father—he's been having a hard time finding a job, and my mother would be devastated if she knew the truth," Archie said.

"Hurting me makes that okay?" I asked.

Archie shook his head. "No. But it was my own version of *Sophie's Choice*."

"I don't think the situations are the same," I said.

"My feelings for you are real." Archie tried grabbing my hand, yet I swatted it away.

Please. Archie couldn't weasel out of this situation that easily. Especially after I gave him an opportunity for honesty when I caught him arguing with Mallory about the weather. At least then, he would've saved Mallory from gloating. But no. Like every other moment of disappointment, I'd just have to live with my churning stomach.

Mallory cackled even louder this time. "I'll leave you guys alone. Sounds like you've got a lot to discuss."

"Wait," I bellowed at Mallory when she started walking away.

"What?" she asked.

"I wanna know why you're intent on hurting me," I said.

Discovering the truth about Mallory's motivation had nothing to do with empathy. If Mallory provided me with an explanation, then I'd stare at my bedroom ceiling a little less each night. I just had to know why she hated me so much—even if I hadn't unclenched my fists. Surely, I wasn't that evil.

"Isn't it obvious?" Mallory asked. "I'm not over you rejecting me at the beginning of the year. We could've been amazing, but no. You had to fall for Archie."

"You're that upset?" I asked.

She snorted. "I'm not taking any chances after Tommy."

No matter how hurt she was from her relationship with Tommy, Mallory had no right to scheme against me. Doing so only continued the cycle of dysfunction. No amount of my pain changed what Tommy did or didn't do to her. So, in a way, life was worse. Instead of one person being hurt, three were now pissed off. And said fact was great—I didn't need to be great at math to know three impacted people was worse than one.

THURSDAY, OCTOBER 25, 2018

Dan, Rebecca, and I went to the local mall a little after noon.

Today was early dismissal day because of some professional development thing for teachers. Except we hadn't made it to the any of the stores. We were currently seated at a table in the food court.

"Thanks again for letting me tag alone even though I'm sure you'd rather be alone," I said.

Rebecca whipped her head back and forth. "Stop with the low self-esteem crap. We enjoy spending time with you, don't we, Dan?"

Dan dunked several fries in ketchup, then finished them in a matter of seconds.

Rebecca elbowed Dan. "You're glad Chad came, right?"

"Absolutely." Dan slurped his soda.

I rested my free hand under my chin. "I'm such an idiot. I had a feeling something was off when Archie wanted to get back together me, yet I fell for it."

Rebecca cringed. "Everyone makes mistakes when it comes to love."

"Not us," Dan said.

Rebecca threw a fry at Dan. "Not helping. The point is, everyone makes mistakes. It's a part of life."

I gave her a mock frown. "Okay, Mom."

"I'm serious," Rebecca said. "I'm sure if I hadn't found Dan, I'd be falling for bad guy after bad guy."

"The worst part is Archie at least feels a little bad whereas Mallory enjoyed every minute of gloating," I said.

"What are you gonna do now?" Dan asked.

"I don't know. I just stormed away from Archie and we haven't talk since," I revealed.

Rebecca exhaled. "I'm not trying to upset you, but you're gonna have to figure out what you wanna do about Archie at some point."

My heart lurched. No matter how much I wished Rebecca was wrong, she wasn't. Something had to be done about Archie if I wanted any sense of sanity. Knowing I had to make a decision and making said decision were different things, though. For a split-second, doing nothing tempted me. At least then the situation couldn't get any worse.

"I know, I know," I said.

"Just know one thing," Rebecca said. "Dan and I will support you no matter what you decide."

"Good to know," I said.

FRIDAY, OCTOBER 26, 2018

Archie approached me in the hallway on my way to first period.

His teeth pricked his lower lip. "We need to talk."

"I have nothing to say."

Yeah. I was in big trouble. There was no right answer when it came to Archie. If I tossed Archie aside, then I lost an opportunity for happiness. But if took Archie back, then I'd judge myself. I would've been the first person to criticize someone for taking back a bad guy.

"I never meant to hurt you," Archie said.

"Did you really just say that?"

"I'm serious. I care a lot about you."

I crossed my arms. "You've got a funny way of showing it."

"Tell me what you want me to do, and I'll do it."

"Some problems don't have easy solutions."

"Making a mistake doesn't mean I deserve eternal damnation," Archie said.

I made a clucking noise with my tongue. "Maybe not. But can you change Mallory having another victory over me?"

He pressed his hands together. "You've gotta believe I'm sorry."

"I don't have to do anything."

"I was a victim too," Archie said. "Mallory still told my mother about my father losing his job."

"Doesn't matter. You should've known better than to play with snakes."

Archie pursed his lips. "Save me the lecture. I know people get bit when they play with snakes."

I made a fist. "You were the first person I slept with."

"I know—I was flattered."

"You don't know how that felt—being so vulnerable with another person," I said.

"Where does this leave us?" Archie demanded.

This conversation was one of those times when "I don't know" was a valid answer.

Deciding what to do about Archie couldn't be rushed, I had to live with what I'd do about him. So, that was why I just drifted through the hallway when the bell rang after another beat. The pain from Archie and

Mallory betraying me again was too much—I almost wished I'd skipped school and stayed in bed. I could only deal with so much crap before not giving a fuck about anything anymore. Enough tears had welled in my eyes over the past couple of days to last several lifetimes.

No matter how much believing in Archie's redemption temped me, Archie wasn't the person I thought he was. And I had no idea what the hell I was supposed to do with that fact. The empty feeling continued growing while I sat down at a desk in back of my first period class.

AFTER

FRIDAY, FEBRUARY 8, 2019

"Sounds like you handled Kelly, so there's no reason to worry," Gemma said.

We stood in an empty hallway before first period. Although the possibility of students walking by wasn't the reason for my constipated face. I didn't understand how Gemma could be so calm. One false move could get Gemma and I in a lot of trouble. Like if my fleeting guilt made me abandon our mission. Or if Gemma betrayed me because Mallory killed Tommy to save me.

"I know, but we need to be careful," I said.

She took her sweater off, then tucked it under her armpit. "You're just overreacting. You couldn't have seriously texted me about chatting just to call off our scheme?"

"No," I stammered.

"Please stop wasting my time and move onto the next step of the plan. We need to get Mallory's locker combination, and Kelly can help. Being Mallory's guardian means she has access to her school account, including her locker combination."

I put my hands on my hips. "I'm aware of that."

"Don't just stand there—do something about it. For better or for worse, you've got a connection with Kelly."

"I want more time."

"I'm tired of waiting," Gemma said.

Having more patience wouldn't have killed Gemma. I risked a lot by helping her, and she could've pretended to be thankful for my assistance. That was what I would've done if roles were reversed. Doing so was the right thing to do—no law or rule required me to scheme with her, yet I was.

I looked down at the floor. "I'm not saying I want to abandon the mission."

"Then what?" Gemma asked.

Yeah. She needed to check her attitude. Annoyance was one thing, but she needed to calm her voice if she wanted me to continue working with her. We wouldn't get anywhere if I recoiled in her presence.

"We should investigate the Parker and Jordon situation."

"That's all the more reason to plant the gun, diary, and flash drive in Mallory's locker."

"Let's talk to Sami—see if she's suspicious about Jordon's death."

Her gaze narrowed. "Do you think Sami wants to chat about the guy who cheated on her? I don't. It'd just upset her."

"I don't care—we're doing this Friday."

"Fine." Gemma pointed her index finger against my chest. "But if you continue stalling, then I'm gonna make your life a living Hell."

"Fair enough."

THURSDAY, FEBRUARY 14, 2019

"I'm glad we did something easy for Valentine's Day," I said.

Archie and I sat at his dining room table—his parents were out of town for several days, so we had the house to ourselves in addition to how Mom said I could sleepover. A white box also rested between us on the linen tablecloth.

Two candles with flames flickering were to the left of the box, yet I didn't chastise Archie. If we were gonna have a corny date, then today was the day. There was something about the lit candles creating an atmospheric setting that almost tricked me into thinking life would be perfect.

"Same," Archie said. "Now let's eat."

I opened the box, and the aroma of cheese, tomatoes, and other herbs lingered in the air. I took two slices just like Archie.

I winced after glancing at my champagne flute.

"Something wrong?" he asked.

"I hope your parents won't be angry with us for drinking their champagne," I said.

"You worry too much. They've got too many bottles in the cellar to notice if a couple of them were consumed."

"Good point."

"I probably shouldn't say this, but I will."

I took my first bite of pizza. "Just tell me—you know my policy about open communication because of everything that's happened to us."

"Are you sure something isn't bothering you?"

How twisted. The universe gave me an opportunity for an honesty, yet I couldn't tell Archie the truth. My reasoning wasn't even because of Archie being disappointed in me—he couldn't complicate a situation that he didn't know anything about.

"I'm fine," I said.

He rubbed my hand. "Good. Anyway, I can't wait for dessert."

"Me too."

The doorbell rang, and I practically jumped out of my chair.

"Are you expecting company?" I asked.

"No."

The doorbell beeped several more times.

"I should see who it is." Archie grabbed a napkin and wiped his lip before rising. He pushed in his chair, then darted out of the dining room.

Deep breaths. No reason to suspect anything was wrong. Something as simple as a package delivery could be the reason for the visitor. It wasn't like Mallory or Gemma would interrupt our date. They had to have better plans—even if that just involved staying home and watching Netflix.

I continued tapping my feet against the wooden floor before standing. Time to check on why Archie was taking so long.

"What's going on?" I demanded after approaching Archie.

Someone giggled, and I shifted my attention. Archie's sister, Andrea, stood by the front door with a suitcase.

"Nice to see you, handsome," Andrea said.

I gave her a skeptical look. "Why are you here?"

"It's simple—I got kicked out boarding school," Andrea said.

Great. As if life wasn't complicated enough working with Gemma or wondering if the police could link Archie, Rebecca, Dan, and I to Tommy's death. I also had to deal with Andrea, because she would've won the award for Sex Crazed Younger Sister—I hadn't forgotten about Christmas Eve and wouldn't. Not if I wanted to protect my relationship with Archie. Any threat to my relationship—whether it was Mallory or someone else—wouldn't be tolerated. Not when I worked so hard to be with Archie.

FRIDAY, FEBRUARY 15, 2019

Gemma and I approached Sami in the school hallway on the way to lunch.

"Do you have a second?" I asked.

She nodded. "Sure. But only a moment—I've got a tutoring appointment."

"We've just been thinking about Jordan a lot in light of Tommy dying," Gemma said.

"I can understand." Sami paused for a second. "What did you wanna ask me?"

"Did you find his death suspicious?" I asked.

Sami tickled her chin with her right index finger. "Drowning was a random way to go considering how he was athletic. But the police couldn't prove someone intentionally drowned him."

"If only," I mumbled.

Sami stole a quick glance at her watch. "I'd love to chat more. Something has never felt right about Jordon's death, but I've gotta go."

"No problem—thanks for helping us," I said.

Sami was soon out of sight, leaving Gemma and me alone.

"Satisfied?" Gemma asked.

"Yes. Anyway, I'll talk to Kelly by Monday."

"You better—otherwise Mallory will be the least of your problems."

Gemma could save her breath—I had every intention of chatting with Kelly. Gemma's anger was one problem I didn't need. The sooner we planted the stuff on Mallory, the sooner we could move on with our lives. Quick closure was the least I deserved, because Mallory had already occupied enough of my thoughts.

MONDAY, FEBRUARY 18, 2019

I knocked on Kelly's office door during one of my free periods, then locked it.

"We need to chat," I said.

She looked up from her computer screen. "I've got nothing to say to you after what you made me agree to."

"Too bad—we're gonna talk whether you want to or not." I shuffled towards the chair in front of Kelly's desk, then sat in it.

"Yes, please join me. It's not like I've gotta prep for my next class."

"I want something from you."

"Besides my time?"

I shot her a menacing glare. "I'm serious, Kelly. I want Mallory's locker combination."

"Not gonna happen."

"You don't wanna argue with me."

"Why? Because you know something about me?" She drew in a breath. "Please. You would've gone to the police if you wanted to take me down."

"I could if I wanted, but I won't."

"Why do you need Mallory's locker combination?" Kelly asked.

I placed my elbows on her desk. "That's how I'm gonna frame Mallory. And no offense, but you aren't bright for someone with a master's degree."

Kelly rolled up her sleeves. "Don't insult me."

Kelly needed to relax—it wasn't like I asked her for both kidneys or a million dollars. She just needed to do this one simple thing for me— something that would benefit both of us despite her refusal to admit so.

"You're right. I'm sorry," I said.

"You still haven't gotten given me a compelling reason to help you."

I sneered. "I know about the inheritance—the one your parents left to Mallory and not you."

"What does that have to do with anything?" she asked.

"Mallory told me about the morality clause—like if she got arrested. The money would revert back to you since you're her only living family."

Kelly cackled. "You really think I'd betray my own sister for money? I've got a stable job, and I'll be fine."

Poor Kelly. The sadness radiating from her eyes revealed something her menacing tone didn't, and I'd use that to my advantage. I only needed a quick survey of pop culture to appreciate how sibling rivalry left deeply engrained scars in some people—scars people pretended didn't exist in hopes of seeming honorable.

"Never hurts to have more money," I said.

"You're despicable."

"You haven't said no, so that reveals more about you than me."

She pouted. "Do you understand what you're asking?"

Damn Kelly. She had to make this situation more difficult, because I would've loved it if she gave me Mallory's locker combination already. She might not have realized my tenacity, but I wouldn't leave her office until I got access to Mallory's locker.

I rolled my eyes. "Mallory could've killed Parker and Jordon. I chatted with Sami, and she wasn't convinced Jordon's death was an accident."

She leaned forward. "I'm not helping you, so leave."

She could channel bravado if she wanted to, but I wouldn't budge. I had a mission and wouldn't stop till it was completed. And Kelly couldn't forget about one important fact—being a writer meant understanding people more than the average person, so I could push all the right triggers. Like psychological warfare as opposed to waterboarding.

"Come on," I said. "You must be pissed your parents left everything to Mallory and not you, and now is your chance to correct your mistake."

"Fine, you're right. Mallory inheriting all that money sucked, and I'd be lying if I said I still didn't think about the issue."

"This problem has a simple solution."

Kelly shook her head. "I give up—you win, and you can have Mallory's locker combination. But I'm not gonna bail you out when this scheme backfires on you."

"Understood."

Kelly grabbed a blue pen and scribbled something down on a post-it. Then, she shoved it in my face. "Now get out of my office!" she exclaimed. "I can't stand the sight of you."

WEDNESDAY, FEBRUARY 20, 2019

I was about to close my locker door when someone clapped their hands over my eyes. Wondering who stood behind me was unnecessary. The deodorant's fruity aroma provided the only clue I needed for guessing who was next to me.

"Thought I'd surprise you," Archie said.

"Mission accomplished."

"How are things with Andrea?"

"You should ask my parents that question."

My lips twitched. "Ouch. That can't be easy. Although I hope you know I'm here if you need me."

"My mom and dad are both pissed and are pleading with the dean to get her back into school despite her failing grades."

"I'm sure everything will be fine."

"Thanks." Archie kissed me on the lips.

High heels clicked against the floor, growing louder with each passing moment. Archie and I soon looked up while the person's grin expanded.

"Can we help you with something?" Archie asked.

"Just spreading the cheer, because it's gonna be a fabulous day. And nothing can change that fact," Gemma said.

I laughed. "Careful, Gemma. You wouldn't want to people to think you're on happy pills."

"Tease me all you want, but just you see. I've got a feeling life is about to get interesting," Gemma said.

"Wishing things into existence must be nice," Archie said.

"I deserve the best of everything," Gemma said.

Someone's screaming cut through the air, and everyone tilted their heads.

Wow. Detective Garrison and Detective Jones hovered by Mallory's open locker with latex gloves on. Detective Garrison held Tommy's father's gun and flash drive while Detective Jones had the diary open to a specific page—possibly the entry about Mallory discovering Gemma and Tommy in bed together.

"I wonder what's happening," Archie said.

"Nothing good," I said.

Gemma adjusted her headband. "Relax. Everything will be fine."

Mallory yelled even louder this time. "You can't go through my locker."

"We can if the school gives us permission because of an anonymous tip indicating you've got a gun on school grounds," Detective Garrison boasted.

Detective Jones stuffed the gun, diary, and flash drive into evidence bags. After that, she and Detective Garrison each grabbed one of Mallory's arm. They then strutted down the hallway while Mallory continued kicking and screaming.

Mallory shifted her head towards me. "Get Kelly. I'm still a minor and can't be questioned without a parent or guardian present."

"Absolutely," I said.

"Nobody can save you from a murder charge," Detective Garrison said before he, Detective Jones, and Mallory disappeared down another hallway.

"This is awful," Archie said, whipping his head back and forth.

Gemma and I exchanged a look.

For a split-second, I almost smirked like Gemma. If even the smallest possibility of never having to deal with Mallory again existed, then I just became five percent happier. Any number of variables could've blown up the situation, yet they hadn't, and I'd cross my fingers the situation continued unfolding in my favor.

148

BEFORE

WEDNESDAY, OCTOBER 31, 2018

Just because I didn't know what I'd do about Archie, didn't mean I didn't know what I'd do about Mallory.

So, yeah. I tapped Mallory's shoulder before first period while she groped through her locker, getting the stuff she needed for first period. Regardless of Mr. Drake's creepiness and theory about Tommy being an "ungrateful shit," I couldn't help still wondering if Mallory was involved in Tommy's disappearance. If she could hurt me over and over—someone who was supposed to be her best friend—then I didn't wanna imagine what she would've done to do someone she dated.

She tilted her head. "What do you want?"

"We need to talk."

"I'm not in the mood for a lecture from you."

"I couldn't care less about what you want."

Mallory huffed after slamming her locker. "Fine. Just say whatever you wanna say."

"I'm declaring war on you."

"Excuse me?" she asked.

"You heard me. I'm done being the victim," I said.

She giggled. "You might wanna practice that a few more times, hon. At least then you'd have more confidence."

"I'm serious, Mallory."

Mallory tugged harder on her slightly frayed backpack strap. "You're gonna have to be more specific."

"I wouldn't be surprised if you had something to do with what happened to Tommy."

Mallory scoffed. "You sound delusional. Maybe I should talk to your mother."

"Nice try Mallory. It doesn't take a genius to realize something isn't adding up. Tommy disappeared within a couple days after your Fourth of July getaway, in addition to his trust fund being drained."

"Have you been chatting with Gemma again?" Mallory asked.

"I don't need to chat with Gemma—I've got a brain that works just fine."

"Yeah, right. There's no way you'd come up with this crap by yourself."

Perhaps I wasn't the only one who should've played poker. At least then Mallory would've bluffed better. People didn't get worked up over simple things, and I could only speculate about what she might've been hiding.

I lifted my brow. "What's wrong? You seem awfully worried for an innocent person."

"I'm not concerned. I just wanna be the one messing with you, not Gemma."

I stepped forward. "Aren't you listening? This isn't about Gemma."

"I had nothing to do with Tommy's disappearance."

She could say that once or a million times, but I wouldn't change my theory. I had nothing to lose from believing Mallory was involved in what happened to Tommy. Doing so gave me something to focus on, because I still wasn't ready to make my decision about forgiving Archie. Not when Mallory's smirk during her revelation remained burned in my mind.

I snickered. "Doubtful. You just don't go from being in love with Tommy to being in love with me."

"Don't flatter yourself."

"You were devastated when I rejected you on the first day of school," I said.

She tucked a lock of hair behind her ear. "You're right—I was disappointed. But that doesn't mean I hurt Tommy."

"One way or another, I'm gonna find out the truth."

"If you ever cared about me, then you'll leave the issue alone," Mallory said.

"I don't think so—not this time."

"What happened to you?" she asked.

Mallory should've known better than to ask her question. After everything Mallory did to me, she couldn't plead stupidity. No thanks. She'd have better luck with tricking a five-year-old into giving her their candy.

"You happened to me. Playing these twisted games doesn't make us friends—it makes us enemies."

"I'll do anything. Just leave it alone," Mallory said.

"Nope."

"I'll apologize for what I did. It wasn't nice of me, and you deserved better."

"Just empty words," I said.

THURSDAY, NOVEMBER 1, 2018

Gravel crunched under my car tires.

My ignition's clunky sound halted when I took my keys out. Then, I exited my car and locked it. I couldn't be too careful—not when I was on a mission.

Traveling to Tommy's lake house after school—about an hour outside of town—was my only option. Even if it meant jimmying the lock with a bobby pin. If I wanted answers about what happened to Tommy, then going to one of the last places he was before disappearing proved my best bet.

Except I didn't count on the neighbor's front door opening, revealing a bald man with a cane stepping onto the front porch.

His lips twitched. "You aren't a member of the Drake family."

Crap. Bitching about the universe always being after me meant I should've anticipated something going wrong. If I didn't do something soon, I'd be in trouble—and I couldn't have that. Being arrested for trespassing wasn't my first choice of college essay topics. No thanks. I didn't deserve a criminal record.

The man folded his arms. "Answer my question."

"I don't mean any harm."

"Give me one good reason not to call the cops. You could be trying to rob the Drake house."

I snarled. "I'm not."

"Fine. Then spill it."

"I'm here to find answers about Tommy."

He rubbed his mustache. "Yeah, I heard about him on the news. What do you wanna know about him?"

"Something doesn't add up."

He chuckled. "What do you mean?"

"I'm not convinced that he's just another bored, runaway teen. Especially because his girlfriend isn't innocent."

The wind whistled, sending a chill through the air. Yet another reminder how fall was winding down and winter's blistering vengeance would arrive before I could count to ten. Like with frost-tinted windows and the acrid stench of smoke drifting through the air from people's wood burning stoves.

His eyes lit up. "I remember her. What a temperamental girl, which was kind of odd for the day after a holiday."

"Would you mind taking a look at something." I pulled up an image of Mallory on my iPhone. Then, I handed my phone to the man after shuffling towards his porch. "Is the girl you're talking about?"

My current formality was one I wouldn't apologize for. If I wanted to accuse Mallory of something, then I had to be sure. Nothing like resembling the emperor with no clothes. No thanks—I had to keep my reputation intact.

He pushed his glasses up his nose, then studied the picture. "Yes, that was her."

"What were they arguing about?" I asked, taking my phone back.

"I'm sorry, but I wasn't paying too much attention to their conversation—I was trying to listen to my morning radio program."

"Anything you can tell?"

He exhaled. "Their argument must've been pretty awful. She screamed at him in the driveway before they left."

"Thank you so much."

"Don't mention it."

"One more thing. Please don't tell anyone about this conversation," I said.

Yeah. I continued my formalness. I read enough mystery books to understand the importance of not leaving myself open to vulnerabilities. Not when there was no telling what Mallory would do if she knew I discovered this nugget of information.

He didn't fret. "Absolutely."

FRIDAY, NOVEMBER 2, 2018

Wind slammed against my house, and the red glow from my alarm clock on the bed board revealed it was a couple minutes before 11:30 P.M.

The weather interrupting my sleep wasn't my biggest problem, though. Nope. The girl sitting next to me on my bed was why my arm hairs stood. I almost screamed when she clapped a hand over my mouth.

"Don't make this any worse than it has to be, because I don't wanna hurt you," Mallory said. "However, we need to get a few things straight."

I rolled my eyes.

"I'll remove my hand if you promise not make a scene and wake your mother," Mallory said. "Can you do that?"

Nodding was my only choice. Fighting with Mallory wasn't worth it—not when my pulse hummed in my ears louder than it ever had before. No telling what Mallory was capable of if she snuck into my house.

"Good," Mallory said. "Anyway, I know you went to Tommy's lake house the other day. But that's the last time you're gonna investigate Tommy's death. Do you understand me?"

Creepy. Mallory actually did it. She hadn't just entered my home past bedtime, she followed me. So, yeah. That burning sensation in my throat the first day of school this year wasn't far-fetched. She was better at stalking than anyone realized—especially if I hadn't realized she tracked me.

"Whatever you say," I replied.

"I'm serious, Chad."

"Fine. I promise to let go of my suspicions."

She bit one of her nails. "Good, because I'd hate to see anything bad happen to you."

Mallory could make all the threats she wanted, yet I wouldn't abandon my search. She didn't have a monopoly on devious behavior. If she was so concerned about what I'd discover, then I was closer to the truth than I realized.

So, yeah. I had no problem cracking a smile. Let her think she won this round. Then, my eventual victory would be even sweeter—the worst defeats were the ones people didn't see coming.

AFTER

WEDNESDAY, FEBRUARY 27, 2019

"Do you think I'm making a mistake by considering a guilty plea?" Mallory asked.

I continued sitting next to Mallory on her bed while moonlight trickled into her bedroom. Forgetting about my scheming with Gemma wouldn't happen anytime soon—not when Mallory wouldn't have been in her current predicament if it wasn't for us. The amount of guilt I'd feel remained to be seen, though. Not punishing myself would've been the smart thing to do if I wanted to enjoy my happily ever after with Archie.

She furrowed her eyebrows. "Well?"

"I can't tell you what to do—it's your life, not mine. Besides, you saved me," I said.

Mallory squeezed my hand. "I'd do it again. Tommy had no right to threaten you."

"But now you might be going to prison."

"Thank goodness for Kelly—I don't know what I would've done if it wasn't for Kelly."

A lump lingered in my throat. "Seriously?"

"I would've cracked if it wasn't for her. But no. She insisted on how I don't know anything, and Tommy and I just had a toxic breakup."

"Was your diary incriminating?" I asked.

"How did you know about my diary?"

Shit. If I wanted to get away with my alliance with Gemma, then I needed to be more discreet. I'd have to think of a quick response if I didn't want my plan unraveling.

"I was there in the hallway when the detectives searched your locker," I said.

She slapped her cheek. "Duh. I'm such an idiot."

My pulse stopped echoing in my ears.

Wow. The universe was on my side for once. I wouldn't have known what I'd do if Mallory hadn't believed my defense. So, yeah. If I continued being careful, then Gemma and I might get away with everything.

"Don't be too hard on yourself—you might lose everything because of me," I said.

"Confessing would solve all of our problems. But to answer your question, no. I stopped writing in my diary after discovering Tommy and Gemma in bed together."

"You don't have to do that."

"Then you won't have to worry about whether I'll ruin your relationship with Archie."

Funny thing for Mallory to say. Some people wouldn't have been so bold with joking about past drama. Denial was always easier than facing the truth—even if the situation involved an enemy.

I frowned "I'm not concerned—Archie and I are stable."

"Even with Andrea back in town?"

"It's gonna take more than his horny sister to ruin our relationship."

"I admire your confidence." Mallory bit her nail. "There's one thing that I could do."

"I don't understand."

"An insanity plea."

The "I don't know" response sometimes proved accurate. It remained to be seen if Mallory going to a mental institution instead of prison would ruin everything Gemma and I planned. Residing in a sanitarium still meant she was locked away. Just not in the way we might've preferred. If the situation reversed itself, then I wouldn't have hesitated about choosing between prison and a mental hospital. The 1800's were a long time ago, and I'd rather have drool on my chin, than always glancing over my shoulders in fear of being raped.

"Why? Do you think the DA would try you as an adult?" I asked.

Mallory shrugged. "I'm not sure, although I can't take the risk. And I'm sure my lawyer wouldn't have mentioned the possibility if he didn't think it was worth it."

I snickered. "I can't believe Kelly got Dave Morrison—he's one of the best defense attorneys in the state."

"Yeah." She pushed a chunk of her hair to the side. "He hasn't lost a case in over two decades."

"It probably doesn't seem like it now, but your life is gonna be okay," I said.

Her head dropped. "One thing bothers me."

Maybe, just maybe, Mallory's therapy turned her into a better person. The old Mallory would've lashed out at me for telling her what to think or for being too positive. But no. She hadn't even winced at my response.

"And what's that?" I asked.

"How the diary, gun, and flash drive got in my locker. Gemma must've broken into my home—I just know it."

"You don't know that."

"Please don't defend Gemma—she's a terrible person and can go to Hell."

"My therapy appointments could help support my insanity defense," Mallory touted.

"That's true."

"I'm sorry to complain—this situation just sucks."

I forced a laugh. "One good thing came from this."

"And what's that?"

"Kelly making arrangements for you to do your assignments from home."

Mallory straightened the bed comforter. "Only because I'd rather die than leave the house."

Kelly knocked on the door. "I don't mean to be a buzzkill, but you should leave, Chad. Mallory needs to start her assignments."

"Can't I have five more minutes with Chad?" Mallory pleaded. "Rebecca and Dan haven't even stopped by to check on me."

Kelly folded her arms. "Trust me. I'm doing you a favor."

Ouch. If I didn't know better, then I would've thought Kelly's comment was a jab at me. And that wasn't fair. No matter how unpleasant helping me might've been, I hadn't been mean to Kelly. I just made her to do something she didn't wanna to do, and she'd have less sleepless nights once she got her inheritance.

I rose. "It's fine; I'll go."

"Smart guy," Kelly said.

"You don't have to leave, Chad," Mallory said.

"Don't worry about me. I'll be fine," I said.

FRIDAY, MARCH 1, 2019

Gemma tapped my shoulder while I stood by my locker, getting everything I needed for my morning classes.

"Excited for the weekend?" I asked.

"Not when Mallory remains free."

"But she's a person of interest."

"Not enough," Mallory said. "I just don't want her to suffer. I wanna witness her eternal damnation."

Yikes. Threatening someone and following through with it were two different things, yet I couldn't shake the contempt in Gemma's eyes. Almost like she'd never be able to sleep again if Mallory went unpunished—there was no telling what she'd be capable of if she didn't get her way.

"I gave everything I had," I said. "It's not my fault if the police need more than circumstantial evidence to arrest her."

She bit her lip. "You're right, and I'm sorry. I just need to keep the faith."

"You could say that again. Increasing the police's suspicion in Mallory is a good thing," I said.

"I'm sure the police will find something eventually."

"How have you been doing?"

Gemma glared at me. "What do you mean?"

"I'm not an idiot—the police must've talked to you in light of the evidence that we planted. People don't just sweep incest under the rug."

She yanked her backpack strap. "Everything is fine. My mom is just making me go to counseling."

Wow. Gemma deserved to win some sort of an award. I wouldn't have had such a calm demeanor if I had an incestuous affair exposed. There was humiliation and then there was live-in-your-bedroom-for-the-rest-of-your-life disappointment. Gemma's parents couldn't have been happy about uncovering the truth regarding Tommy and Gemma. Incest didn't have a positive spin no matter how optimistic someone was.

"You aren't worried about being thrown in foster care or something?" I asked.

"I might or might not have threatened the detectives."

"I'm impressed," I said.

"No need for praise—I did what needed to be done."

"She's considering an insanity plea to make her life easier."

"How do you know?" Gemma asked.

"I visited her Wednesday night."

"Not sure that's the best idea. You might end up feeling guilty."

"I can handle myself."

"Whatever you say." Gemma remained silent for a moment. "Anyway, I wouldn't be mad about Mallory going to a sanitarium."

Interesting. I would've suspected Gemma would be furious if Mallory wasn't locked away for the rest of her life. Then again, Gemma might've been that desperate about wanting Mallory gone. So, she might've welcomed anything that banished Mallory.

I raised my eyebrows. "Really?"

"Mallory just needs to disappear at this point."

Okay. Good to know I still had a future as a psychic. I could always count on my intuition no matter how unpredictable life was.

"Good to know," I said.

Footsteps shuffled, getting louder with each passing moment. Then, Archie scowled at me. "What's going on, babe?" he asked before kissing me.

"Gemma and I were discussing an assignment," I said.

Gemma didn't blink. "I was confused about something, but I get it now."

"Whatever," Archie said.

Perhaps gullible behavior was contagious. First Mallory believed the diary excuse and now Archie bought my explanation for why Gemma and I were talking.

MONDAY, MARCH 4, 2019

I closed my textbook and notebook while sitting at a table in back of the cafeteria during one of my free periods. Then, I stuffed them into my backpack.

Archie accosted me. "We need to talk."

Fantastic. He just said the one thing every teenager dreamed of hearing, and I couldn't wait to hear what he had to say.

"What's up?" I asked.

He threw a gaze towards an adjacent hallway. "Not here."

"Everything okay?" I asked once we stepped into the hallway.

"I kept thinking about your conversation with Gemma."

Shit. This conversation couldn't have been headed in the direction I thought it was. Even the universe couldn't have been that cruel on a Monday morning.

"I explained that to you. We were talking about a homework assignment," I said.

"I've seen you chatting with Gemma several times over the last few weeks." Archie sucked in a breath. "And I know what happened."

"You do?"

Yeah. If Archie was gonna make an accusation, then he had to actually say it. I wouldn't make the situation any easier for him. Not when my relationship might've been seconds away from unraveling.

"At first, I suspected Gemma of planting those things in Mallory's locker—Mallory might be vindictive but she's not stupid," Archie said. "But I think she had help."

"What's your point?" I asked.

"You helped her, didn't you? You knew about Mallory's diary entry about uncovering Tommy and Gemma's affair in addition to how Kelly put the gun and flash drive in her safe."

Fuck it. Maybe trying something unexpected was what would save my relationship with Archie.

My nostrils flared. "Congratulations, you're right. I teamed up with Gemma."

Several students walked by while Archie remained silent, and I couldn't wait for the next thing out of Archie's mouth.

"You better have a good explanation for your behavior," he said.

BEFORE

MONDAY, NOVEMBER 5, 2018

Afternoon sunlight trickled into Mallory's bedroom while I was standing in front of her desk.

Yup. Somehow, I was gonna end my feud with Mallory by gaining the upper hand over the Tommy situation. Even if I had no idea what my sleuthing would uncover. There was no forgetting my twitching jaw when Mallory snuck into my bedroom and demanded I back off about Tommy. If didn't know better, then I would've accused her of being unhinged.

I didn't have to worry about Mallory finding me, though. She was in New York for the afternoon with the high school's debate team and Kelly let me in the house under the premise of returning a book Mallory lent me.

I placed Mallory's copy of *Gone Girl* on her desk, then did a 180 of her room. Whatever my search entailed, I had to be discreet. There was no telling how Mallory would react if she realized I snooped through her bedroom.

Something caught my attention from the corner of my eye. A leather journal poked out from a stack of papers and books on Mallory's desk. I only had one option—time to read Mallory's diary.

I snatched the diary from the clutter, then flipped through it.

I paused on one entry while my pulse continued drumming in my ears. I couldn't have read what I just had—an entry from the beginning of last June. But I wasn't having a fever dream, which meant accepting what I discovered. Even if said detail defied societal norms.

No matter how much rage pulsed through my body from Mallory's behavior since the beginning of September, I now understood what was wrong with her. And maybe, just maybe, I would've empathized with Mallory if it wasn't for her blackmailing Archie into an indecent proposal. I would've been angry if I discovered my boyfriend in bed with his sister, because there was no excusing Tommy and Gemma sleeping together.

I could speculate even if I needed more facts before accusing Mallory of murder. Discovering Tommy and Gemma's affair provided a motive for harming Tommy. I might not have paid much attention in freshman English, yet I remembered the bit about nothing like a scorned woman.

Shuffling footsteps grew louder and louder.

Crap. Kelly might've been coming to check on me.

I shoved Mallory's diary back under the pile of clutter on her desk, then forced a smile when Kelly entered the bedroom.

She giggled. "You're taking a while to return a book."

"I was feeling nostalgic."

"Excuse me?" she asked.

"I regret my strained relationship with Mallory."

"Dynamics change."

"Doesn't mean I have to like it," I said.

"Count yourself lucky," Kelly said. "You were her friend, not her sister, so you aren't obligated to have her in your life."

I smirked. "Do I detect resentment?"

"You said it; I didn't."

WEDNESDAY, NOVEMBER 7, 2018

Water gushed from the bathroom sink, then I splashed it into my face.

Deep breaths. I had a few minutes before first period and could pretend life was okay. Nobody else had to know today was my father's birthday just because I did.

I turned the faucet off and grabbed a paper towel from the dispenser to the left of the sink. After that, I wiped my face.

The door creaked, revealing a guy.

Archie grinned. "Funny seeing you here."

"Hi," I mumbled.

He elevated his eyebrows. "Something wrong?"

"Just normal school worries."

Archie crossed his arms. "Try again. Even I'm not that gullible."

"I'm not discussing this with you."

"I still care about you."

I snorted. "It's a little late for that."

"Don't be like this. Give me another chance to prove myself."

My lips curled. The universe shouldn't have tested me, yet here I was. And I'd have to guard the secret about today being my father's birthday. Archie didn't have a right to see me vulnerable after agreeing to Mallory's indecent proposal.

"Come on." He inched forward, so close his breath prickled against my skin. "What's the worst that'll happen from an honest conversation?"

I grunted. "Fine. Have it your way."

"Spill it."

"Today would've been my father's forty-second birthday," I said.

He shuddered. "I had no idea."

"I should go." I was about to leave when Archie grabbed my arm, sending chills up my back. No matter how much time passed, the spark was still there. The spark that left my mouth gaped. If Archie hadn't hurt me, then I would've wanted to kiss him. There was no point in our lips being so close to each other if we weren't gonna do anything about it.

"We can ditch school if you want," Archie said.

"I'm not in the mood to get in trouble."

He extended his arm and parted a lock of my hair to the side. "You've got no reason to believe me, but I really am sorry about everything."

"Archie, please!"

"If I could do everything over, things would be so different."

"What's done is done."

"If you won't talk about your pain with me, then you should chat with Rebecca and Dan. I'm sure they'd be happy to listen."

"I'll think about it."

His eyes remained glued to mine. "You don't deserve to be unhappy—you deserve the best of everything."

"I've learned to live with the pain like everything else in life."

"Fuck it." Archie pulled me up against his body, then kissed him. He even buried his fingers in my hair and gave me tongue.

I didn't push him away, though. I let him continue kissing me while closing my eyes. Things weren't often mutually exclusive in life. I could be pissed with Archie but still wanna kiss him. While I might not have been sure of much, I had this moment, and I'd enjoy it while I could. Especially when I had no idea what I'd do about the Gemma and Tommy revelation.

THURSDAY, NOVEMBER 8, 2018

Rebecca and I hovered in front of Dan's locker before first period.

"I wish Thanksgiving would arrive already," Dan said.

Rebecca glared, then rubbed her eye. "You've got some time before that."

"Don't kill a dream," Dan said.

Archie drifted down the hallway, giving me a look. I met his gaze before he was soon out of sight.

"What was that about?" Rebecca sipped from her water bottle.

"You don't wanna know," I said.

Dan closed his locker. "Yeah, we do. Keeping secrets is rude."

Fine. Time for me to reveal the truth. Perhaps getting their perspective would provide insight into what I was supposed to do about Archie. I could hope, at least. Needing advice was natural, even if I had to live for me, not anyone else.

"We kissed yesterday," I blurted.

Rebecca's eyes almost popped out of their sockets. "What?"

"It was my father's birthday," I said.

Dan's Adam's apple bobbed. "That's right…"

"I'm sorry we weren't there for you," Rebecca said.

I exhaled. "No point in complaining about it now."

"We should've been more considerate, and it won't happen again," Rebecca said.

Dan nodded. "Absolutely."

"Do you know what you're gonna do about Archie?" Rebecca asked.

Way to ask a loaded question. I had no clue how I was supposed to talk about my feelings with other people if I couldn't acknowledge them to myself. Especially if I'd always wonder when the next thing would go wrong in my relationship with Archie. No telling what Mallory was capable of doing anymore.

TUESDAY, NOVEMBER 13, 2018

I trekked through the school hallway on the way to lunch when I bumped into Archie.

"Doing better?" he asked.

"Yeah. It was just a bad day."

"Glad to hear it."

"I didn't mean to dump on you."

Archie shook his head. "Please don't apologize, Chad."

"I hope I didn't send mixed signals by not stopping the kiss."

"Don't worry about it—I shouldn't have kissed you during your moment of vulnerability," Archie said.

I took in a breath. "I wanted to kiss you."

"Really?"

"Running into you is good—I was gonna find you anyway."

He wiggled his eyebrows. "I'm not that hard to find—we've got several classes together."

"I know, I know."

"Is there any way you can give me another chance?" Archie pleaded.

Bad things would happen regardless of if Archie was in my life. I also couldn't let Mallory win the "game." I deserved the opportunity to pursue my own happiness. If Archie and I were gonna make our relationship work, then we actually had to try. No bullshit. No lies. No secrets. It was one hundred percent, or it was nothing.

I laughed. "Fine. You're on probation."

"What does that mean?"

"I'll give you a chance to prove yourself, but don't make me regret it."

"I won't."

The bell rang.

"Would you wanna grab lunch together?" he asked.

I didn't hesitate—not even for a second. "Sure. That'd be great."

Archie grabbed my hand and we darted down the hallway. Having lunch together wouldn't eliminate my skepticism of Archie, but it was a start, and I wouldn't dismiss the opportunity to build a better future. If I wanted to improve my life, then I had to believe happiness was possible.

FRIDAY, NOVEMBER 16, 2018

Archie and I stood in my kitchen a little past eight in the evening.

Mom was away on a business trip for the weekend, and Archie and I'd take advantage of the alone time. No telling when we'd have the opportunity again, because I so wanted Mom to walk in on us and give us a sex talk.

I handed Archie a bowl. "Enjoy!"

"I will. Espresso chip is my favorite flavor of ice cream."

I was about to take a bite of my ice cream when something beeped.

I couldn't help but check my phone when hanging out with Archie, even if some people thought doing so was rude. I was still a teenager, and Mom might've wanted to check in on me. I couldn't let her worry. Pointless drama was the last thing I needed. My life was supposed to be getting less complicated, not more complicated.

I grumbled after sneaking a peak at my iPhone. I had one new text message from Mallory: *I'm so sorry for everything and I hope you'll think of me fondly one day.*

"What's wrong?" Archie demanded.

"Nothing."

"It wasn't nothing."

"You're right—the text was from Mallory," I said.

"What happened to no more secrets?" Archie finished the rest of the ice cream, then placed the bowl in the sink.

"Mallory doesn't matter. Nothing is gonna spoil our evening," I said.

"If you say so. What did she want?"

"See for yourself." Handing Archie my iPhone was best. It wasn't like he wanted to track my every move—he was just a little curious. And if I wanted him to be open with me, then I needed to lead by example.

His lips quivered. "You aren't worried about Mallory?"

"No," I said, taking my iPhone back from him.

Archie put his hands on his hips. "How can you be so sure?"

"She always pulls crap like this." I remained silent for a second. "Like last May when she got into a fight with her sister, Kelly, and made everyone think she was missing for a couple days."

"If you say so."

"Enough about Mallory. How about we go watch that movie?" I asked.

"Sure."

Yup. No need for guilt. Mallory actually hadn't said she'd harm herself, so I could pretend she was fine. She also wasn't my responsibility after everything she put me through. If she had a problem, then she could bitch to her sister. Kelly was the only one who was obligated to tolerate Mallory's crap, and that was just the way it was.

SATURDAY, NOVEMBER 17, 2018

Archie and I exited Starbucks while not much blue remained in the afternoon sky.

The universe was once again in the mood to fuck with us, though. Mallory just left the sandwich shop a couple of feet away from us. However, she didn't have her typical hyena smile. Instead, her face drooped. Almost as if she hadn't been faking it yesterday when she texted me.

Archie leaned into my ear. "Should we say something?"

"No," I said, whipping my head back and forth. "Let's just get dinner."

Mallory hollered at us when we were about to walk away. "How are you guys doing?" she asked.

"Fine," I said.

Mallory played with a strand of her hair. "What are you up to?"

"Just gonna grab a bite to eat, then watch some Netflix," Archie said.

Mallory frowned at me. "I tried reaching out to you yesterday."

I squeezed Archie's hand tighter. "We were busy."

"I'm really sorry for everything that's happened and would like a fresh start," Mallory said. "I don't wanna fight with you anymore, Chad."

Hell must've frozen over. Mallory didn't have a wrinkled nose, and I once again almost believed she was being honest. She had nothing to gain at this point—more scheming would only make me hate her more.

Intellectualizing how she was young enough to start over didn't mean I should've been the one to give her a second chance. Forgiving her wouldn't erase everything she did to me. I might not have been perfect, yet I had never done anything as bad as Mallory.

The wind rattled through the air, and my teeth chattered. So much for hoping the cold weather wouldn't arrive.

"I'd really like some company tonight," Mallory said. "Kelly is out with her girlfriends, and it'd nice to do something fun."

"And why should we do that? Nothing requires us to be friends," I said.

Mallory pushed up her sleeves. "You'd want someone to give you another chance if you were in my position. Also, I can spring for a bottle of tequila because of my fake ID."

No matter how much I almost kicked myself for considering the possibility, I wouldn't. Being "friends" with Mallory provided an opportunity to dig for more information on Tommy. I'd beat her at her own game.

"Fine. We're gonna go eat, but you can meet us at my house at eight," I said.

"Great. You won't regret this," Mallory said.

Archie, Mallory, and I sat on my bedroom floor a little past eight with the bottle of tequila in the middle of us.

Mallory took a swig of tequila, then glanced at me. "I want a real answer about why you never pursued something with me."

"Some people are only meant to be friends," I said.

"But you're bisexual," Mallory said.

"That doesn't mean I wanna sleep with everyone," I said.

Archie let out a loud laugh yet didn't say anything. Instead, his face turned bright red.

"What's so funny? I asked.

"You're gonna have to kiss Mallory to shut her up," Archie said.

"That's a terrible idea." I yanked the tequila bottle away from Mallory and took a more than generous swig of it.

Mallory giggled. "It's perfect. If you kiss me and honestly don't feel anything for me, then I'll never mention the issue again."

My heart almost leapt out of my chest. Getting answers about Tommy shouldn't have meant pimping myself out, yet I didn't have a choice. Not when I had to do whatever it took to keep Mallory happy. And if she promised never to mention rejecting me again, then that was also a bonus.

I cocked my head. "You're okay with this?"

"I'm all about love," Archie said. "I also need to be honest with you two—I care about both of you."

Whether the tequila caused Archie's bluntness didn't matter. He couldn't take back what he just said, so I'd once again just have to live with something.

Mallory winked. "What are you waiting for, Chad? It's about time you showed me why Archie gets all hot and bothered over you."

"Fine." I scooted towards Mallory, and she made the first move. The kiss lasted for a few seconds before we pulled away.

"Well?" Mallory demanded.

I shrugged. "It was a kiss."

Mallory jabbed my shoulder. "Admit it. You felt something."

"Fess up," Archie said, slurring his words.

"Fine. It wasn't terrible, but that doesn't mean it should happen again," I said.

Mallory's eyes lit up. "You said it shouldn't, not that you don't want it to."

"Drink your tequila," I said.

Mallory smacked her hands together, and I could only wonder what idea she just concocted. "I know what will make this night more exciting—a threesome."

"That's okay," I said.

"Don't be so uptight," Archie said.

I sucked in a breath. "We've been drinking."

"Being drunk doesn't mean we aren't attracted to each other," Mallory said. "Let's go for it."

"I'll pass," I said, raising my voice.

Mallory eyed Archie. "What do you say?"

"I'm game," Archie replied. "Now the only question is if you are, Chad?"

Just because Mallory wasn't ugly didn't mean I should've agreed to her proposition—actions had consequences, and the morning after a threesome would bring all sorts of awkwardness, I might not have been ready for. Yet I still wanted to take Mallory down, and would do whatever it took. Even if I had to sleep with her. It wasn't like someone put a gun to my head. And I also couldn't forget about Archie—he seemed keen on this threesome, and I couldn't lose him.

"Fine. But we are never ever gonna discuss the threesome after tonight," I said.

174

AFTER

SUNDAY, MARCH 10, 2019

Archie, Dan, Rebecca, Mallory, and I were in Mallory's living room a little past four in the afternoon.

Someone hadn't blackmailed us all to be in the same location, though. Mallory's lawyer got her an insanity plea bargain, and Mallory was scheduled to turn herself into the police tomorrow morning at 9:00 a.m. And Kelly somehow agreed to let us have a party so long as we agreed not to get rowdy or leave the house.

Mallory tapped my shoulder while I stood in front of the table, pouring my tequila into my red Solo cup. Then, I mixed it with seltzer. "Everything okay?" she asked.

I chuckled. "I should be asking you that considering what tonight is."

"I'm not angry," Mallory said. "If I'm gonna be a person of interest, then I might as well take control of the situation."

"That's big of you."

Mallory glanced at the other end of the living room—more specifically, Archie. He remained engrossed in conversation with Rebecca and Dan.

"Everything okay with you and Archie?" she asked.

I took a swig of my cocktail. "Why would you ask me that?"

"You two arrived separately, in addition to how you haven't said one word to each other."

"Dynamics change."

"Did you break up?" Mallory asked, lowering her voice.

"It's a complicated situation."

She jabbed my shoulder, and I almost spilled my drink. "Give me the details. It'd make me feel better."

"I thought you were okay with the arrangement?"

"Only because it spares you, Rebecca, Dan, and Archie." Mallory brought her glass up to her nose, then swirled the contents. After that, Mallory finished her remaining wine in one gulp. "Now tell me what's going on with you and Archie."

"This isn't celebrity gossip—it's my life."

She sighed. "Sorry, I didn't mean it that way."

"Please. You've never been happy about my relationship with Archie." I took a bigger sip this time.

"Where's this coming from?" Mallory refilled her wine glass from the bottle on the table. "I thought we were in a good place?"

"Fine. I'll keep my opinion to myself."

"You're right. I should apologize," Mallory said. "I should never have come between you and Archie. And I now understand how our threesome was a big mistake."

I did a 180 around the living room. Dan, Rebecca, and Archie remained engrossed in conversation. "We agreed not to talk about that night," I said.

Yeah. Mallory should've gotten to the point like yesterday. I couldn't think of a good reason to discuss our threesome. Not now. not ever.

"I knew your opinion of me wouldn't change even if you slept with me. Yet I went along with it," Mallory said.

"I wanna know one thing."

"Shoot."

"Why were you so desperate for me to love you?" I asked.

"Having anything to focus on was better than thinking about Tommy and Gemma."

"You were that upset?"

Mallory gripped her neck. "Can you blame me? It hasn't even been a year since Parker cheated on me."

Parker. Couldn't forget about the name even if I tried. I'd always wonder if Mallory might've had something to do with his and Jordon's deaths thanks to Kelly's newspaper clippings. Similar causes of death weren't something I could forget about by snapping my fingers, proving how knowledge was more of a curse than a blessing.

Archie grumbled at me after shuffling towards the table. "Excuse me."

I stepped to the left, and Archie grabbed more ice before pouring whiskey and Diet Coke into his cup.

Mallory snorted. "You suck, Archie."

"You couldn't be more wrong. Did you know I'm on your side for once?" Archie took a more than generous sip of his cocktail.

"You and Archie are good together and it'd be a shame for you to throw away your relationship over a silly fight," Mallory said.

Having Mallory support my relationship with Archie at the most inconvenient time was exactly what the universe would do. If it gave me something good, then it'd be in the most ridiculous way possible.

Archie's pupils dilated. "Did Chad tell you why we broke up?"

"No, but I'm sure it was for a stupid reason," Mallory said.

"Weren't you paying attention to what I said?" Archie asked, speaking louder. "I'm on your side, so you should be thanking me."

"I'm not following you," Mallory said.

Archie shot me a glance. "Do you wanna tell her, or should I?"

"There's nothing to tell," I said.

My back hairs rose. If Archie knew what was best, then he'd drop the topic. Nothing good would come from Archie outing what he knew about my scheme with Gemma.

Archie shrieked. "Bullshit. And it's hypocritical of you to be here in light of what you and Gemma did to Mallory."

Rebecca and Dan looked towards Archie, Mallory, and me.

"Will someone please tell me what's going on?" Mallory asked.

"Gladly," Archie said.

"Please don't do this—you wouldn't if you ever loved me," I said to Archie.

"Too late," Archie said. "Mallory is gonna know about the real you whether you like it or not. Actions have consequences, and you're about to face yours."

"Enough stalling," Mallory said.

"Chad worked with Gemma and they planted the gun, diary, and flash drive in your locker," Archie revealed.

"You're saying that because you're drunk," Mallory said.

"Ask Chad yourself," Archie said.

Fuck it. No point in denying my plan—it wasn't like Mallory could do anything about it. The police and DA would've only thought she was crazy. And maybe, just maybe, I was entitled to a little fun. Scheming wouldn't have been worth it if I couldn't gloat.

I placed my cup on the table, then grunted. "Archie isn't lying. I worked with Gemma to take you down. You deserved it after everything you did."

Mallory screamed. "Have you forgotten you'd be dead if I hadn't killed Tommy?"

"That doesn't mean I'm in debt to you for the rest of my life," I said.

"You could show some gratitude, though." Mallory shook her head. "I'm not gonna argue with you again. I'm just gonna go to my room and think."

Mallory went up the living room staircase and was soon out of sight.

"You should be ashamed of yourself," I said.

"Don't put this on me," Archie said.

I scoffed. "Tell me something. Do you feel good about dropping your bombshell?"

"Yeah, I do," Archie said.

Dan and Rebecca walked over to Archie and me. Except Archie's wrath might not have been my only problem—Rebecca couldn't stop glaring at me.

"Please tell me this is a misunderstanding?" Rebecca asked.

"I did what I had to do, and I'm not gonna apologize." I grabbed my cup, then chugged the rest of my drink and belched. After that, I crushed the cup and it fell onto the floor. "I should go check on Mallory before she does something stupid.

I scurried up the staircase, then ran towards Mallory's bedroom.

The door was open, so I didn't bother knocking.

Mallory wasn't in her bedroom and her backpack was no longer on her bed. I couldn't forget about the chill permeating the air—the bedroom window was opened.

Wow. I just couldn't believe Mallory escaped her own goodbye party.

I darted over to the window. There was less than a ten-foot drop from the window to the garden below. So, maybe, just maybe that was how Mallory fled—stranger things happened all the time. The ivy growing on the side of the house might've also provided a cushion.

WEDNESDAY, MARCH 13, 2019

I blocked Archie in the hallway after running into him on the way to lunch.

"I'm tired of not talking," I said.

"I've got nothing to say."

"Either we're together or we're not, but you can't have it both ways."

He smiled. "Fine. We're done."

"You can't end our relationship without a real conversation."

Caring about seeming blunt didn't matter. I'd do whatever it took to save my relationship with Archie. I wouldn't let anything stand in the way of my happiness—especially since we didn't have to worry about

Mallory. She still hadn't been found, and the police had an APB out on her.

Archie expelled a laugh. "I just did."

"You're being unfair," I said.

"You can't force me to be in a relationship."

"Can't you understand why I schemed with Gemma?" I asked. "It was because I didn't want anything jeopardize our future."

"You did that all on your own."

Perhaps I misjudged Archie. I never once considered him to be cruel, yet how he could defend Mallory was beyond me. Especially because the situation involved more than my hurt feelings. Mallory risked his parents' marriage with the leverage about his father losing his job.

"Have you forgotten what Mallory did to me?" I spat.

"That doesn't justify framing her."

"She actually killed Tommy." I remained silent for a beat, drawing in a breath. "And have you forgotten about what you've done? Like your indecent proposal you agreed to last fall?"

"That's in the past."

"That proves you aren't perfect—you did that to protect your father just like I wanted to protect our future."

"Please don't compare the two situations."

"There's something you don't know," I blurted.

"Nothing changes what you did."

"It's about something that happened with Tommy a few weeks before the start of freshman year."

I sat on the floor with my back pressed against my bed a couple weeks after I turned fifteen. It was several weeks before I'd start high school and Tommy happened to be seated next to me.

I just closed my laptop—we finished watching a Netflix film—and Tommy hadn't stopped looking into my eyes.

"Something wrong?" I asked.

"I was curious about something."

"Ask away—I've got nothing to hide."

"Was coming out as bisexual difficult?" Tommy asked.

"Why would you ask that?"

"I just wanted to know if your life has gotten more challenging."

"No. I couldn't be happier."

"I'm gonna do something but you've gotta promise not to freak out," Tommy said, stuttering.

"Okay."

Tommy kissed me before I caught my breath, yet I didn't push him away. I even let him shove his tongue in my mouth before we pulled away from each other a moment later.

"What was that about?" I asked.

"I wanted to know what kissing a guy felt like."

If only I was high—Tommy couldn't have said what he had. Guys like Tommy were supposed to end up with models for girlfriends. I'd also never once detected a "not-straight" vibe from Tommy.

"Well, you got your answer," I said.

"There's something else I want, but I wasn't sure if you'd agree."

"You'll never know unless you ask."

Tommy's eyes beamed. "Would you consider sleeping with me once? It'd clear up some confusion."

"I've never slept with anyone before," I said.

Wow. At least now I understood where the expression "stranger than fiction" came from. Some events were too unusual to make up. Tommy wanting to sleep with me just couldn't be rationalized no matter what way I looked at the situation.

He stroked my chin, and a tingling sensation shot through my fingers. "I promise you'll be safe—I won't hurt you."

"I don't know…"

"You'd be doing me a favor."

"You're gonna have to try harder if you wanna seduce me."

I lifted my head off Tommy's chest sometime later, then scooted right. No explanation necessary about how this moment would end sooner rather than later, so I might as well have been the one to end it.

Tommy craned his neck. "Something wrong?"

"I just like my personal space."

"I kept my promise—I didn't hurt you."

"There's a difference between physically injured and emotionally injured."

He sat up in bed, keeping his half of the bed comforter wrapped around him. "You answered a lot of my questions. However, I want you to know this doesn't change anything, and you'll always remain my best friend."

Please. Tommy's response was what people always said before ghosting or gutting someone like a fish.

Several teachers and students shuffled down the hallway while Archie sighed at me. "I'm sorry Tommy cut you out of his life after you slept together, but that isn't my fault," he said.

"I didn't do anything wrong—Tommy begged me to sleep with him."

"I should be even angrier at you."

I crossed my arms. "Why?"

"You lied about being a virgin."

"It's not like I know your entire sexual history."

"True. But I never claimed to be something I wasn't."

A silence ensued. For once, I didn't know what I'd do. Nothing I said changed the situation, and Archie and I might've been done for real.

How ironic. My reasoning for scheming was what might end my relationship with Archie and I now had another chapter to add to my memoir about how the universe enacted its twisted sense of humor on me.

He pressed his hands together. "Breaking up isn't about punishing you—it's about not liking the person that saving our relationship turned you into."

"You just don't get it," I said, screaming. "I had to do whatever it takes to protect our relationship because I wasn't about to lose something for a second time."

"I'm looking out for you, Chad. Dating me shouldn't make you compromise your character."

THURSDAY, MARCH 14, 2019

I sobbed while sitting in an empty hallway during lunch.

Shoes clicked against the ground, and I lifted my gaze. Perfect. An impromptu Gemma sighting would brighten my day.

"If you're gonna ask me about Mallory, then save your breath." I rubbed my eyes. "I already told the police I've got no idea where she is."

"Have you been crying?"

"You must know about my breakup with Archie."

"That can't be easy." Gemma slouched onto the ground next to me.

"Archie is something else."

"I'm sure he'll calm down eventually," Gemma said.

I hissed. "He didn't care about my reasoning."

"You mean about protecting your relationship?"

"Yes, but there's more behind my motivation."

"Because Tommy ditched you after your afternoon of experimentation?"

I almost choked. "You know about that?"

"Mallory isn't the only one who kept a diary—Tommy did as well. Journaling was his way of coping with our father." Gemma coughed into her right arm. "That's also why I haven't been harder on you."

"You don't hate me?" I asked.

"Tommy's dead, and nothing changes that fact."

I once again shouldn't have been surprised by the universe's sense of humor. Whether unorthodox or not, I wouldn't push Gemma away. Not when she was the only person offering me unconditional support.

BEFORE

TUESDAY, NOVEMBER 27, 2018

I roamed through the school hallway before first period on the way to my locker, crossing paths with Mallory.

She glared at me. "We need to talk."

"Something wrong?"

"Don't play stupid with me." Mallory grabbed me by my shirt collar and dragged me into a nearby hallway. Then, she shoved me against the wall.

"What's wrong?" I stammered.

"I know you took it."

"You're gonna have to be more specific."

"My flash drive with a videotape is missing," Mallory snapped, arms gripping my collar tighter.

"You've lost me."

Mallory snarled. "This isn't funny, Chad. You've got no idea how sensitive the video is."

She needed a lesson in decorum like yesterday. If Mallory wasn't careful, then I'd think she was even more unhinged than she already was. And that possibility was great. I so dreamed of her sneaking into my bedroom again. Doing it once wasn't enough, and I was determined to traumatize myself again.

"Why I am your first suspect?" I asked.

"You hate me so much that you'd use what's on the tape against me."

"You've lost it."

Mallory grunted. "You don't wanna mess with me."

"Okay. Let's say I stole the flash drive. Wouldn't I have already made my demand by now?"

"Fine." She released me. "But I still don't trust you."

"The feeling is mutual."

She pushed up her sleeves. "You and Archie are the ones who cut me off after the threesome."

If only Mallory hadn't brought up the threesome. Just like I wanted her to surprise me, I also hoped to relive every grueling moment of that Saturday night.

Like me stroking her hair before laying her down on the bed and having my way with her while Archie watched. Or observing while Archie had his turn and I oozed of jealousy. Sobriety wasn't required for realizing how that night was a bad idea. If I had to do it again, then I wouldn't have agreed to the tryst. Alienating Archie wasn't worth discovering the truth about Tommy and bringing down Mallory.

Worse still, was when I lay on my stomach with Archie, hands touching while he leaned against me. Envy was one thing when I experienced it, yet the emotion was worse when the possibility of Mallory losing it lurked in the back of my mind. Like in the school hallway when she spied on my first conversation with Archie.

I sighed. "We've talked to you since then."

"One lunch and a few words isn't much."

"Did you forget about Thanksgiving?" I asked.

"That was only last Thursday and Friday."

"And Saturday and Sunday," I interrupted.

She pursed her lips. "Don't get cute."

"I'm sorry you're upset, but I can't help you."

"I'm gonna be watching you. And don't forget something. If I used Archie as a weapon against you once, then I can do it again."

I chuckled. "You wouldn't do that—not this time."

"And why is that?" Mallory demanded.

"You wouldn't blow our truce—you'd have nobody if you did."

Several students darted by us while Mallory remained silent for a moment.

Good to know she had some standards, because I so wanted to get into trouble or have the whole school gossip and speculate about fighting with Mallory.

She wrinkled her nose. "If you didn't steal the flash drive, then I wanna know who did. I just gotta get that video back."

Wow. The video must've been important. I never once witnessed someone get so worked up over a flash drive before.

Wait. Perhaps the video was more serious than I realized. Only one thing made Mallory more worked up then me rejecting her—Tommy and Gemma. More specifically, their affair. I hadn't forgotten how she wrote in her diary about wishing she could've killed them.

So maybe, just maybe, the video could've been of Tommy and Gemma having sex. Although I would've liked to know what happened to Tommy and his trust fund. They couldn't have vanished into thin air.

WEDNESDAY, NOVEMBER 28, 2018

Dan, Rebecca, Archie, and I went to the Spindlewood Diner for dinner—a restaurant a couple of towns away.

Rebecca shifted her weight in the booth. "This was a great idea—I'm so glad we're going on a double date."

Dan's eyebrows swung upward. "This was your idea."

"It doesn't mean it was a bad idea," Rebecca said.

"No need to toot your own horn," Dan said.

"Doesn't matter. The important thing is we're here," I said.

Archie laughed. "Has anyone told you how you fight like an old married couple?"

Rebecca gasped. "That's not true."

"It was a compliment," Archie said.

"Fine." Rebecca turned to the menu's next page. "Anyway, I have no idea what I wanna order."

"We can always ask for more time," Dan said. "I doubt it'll be a big deal."

Dan was right. The echoing of numerous voices was the only hint we needed for realizing how crowded the place was and nobody would take our order for a little while longer. I was pretty sure there wasn't a free seat in the entire diner. So, yeah. We'd be fine. It wasn't like Mallory just arrived and accused one of us of stealing the flash drive.

Damn. Mallory was an issue even when she wasn't physically present, because I loved cringing from trying to anticipate what her next move would be. It wasn't like she ever overreacted before.

Archie eyed me. "Something wrong?"

"No. I'm just tired," I said.

Rebecca closed her menu. "I'm gonna get a salad."

"You could make that at home," Dan said.

Perhaps Archie had a point.

Sure. Nothing wrong with debating friends. But I wouldn't have wanted to be with someone who turned every little thing into a discourse. Life was too short, and there were more important aspects to focus on.

"I don't feel like getting anything fancy," Rebecca said.

Dan rolled his eyes. "Whatever you say."

"Tell me again about how you two don't resemble an old married couple?" Archie asked.

"Okay." Rebecca undid her ponytail, letting her hair free. "You might have a point. But I don't wanna think about getting old for a long time."

"There are worse things in life than old age," Archie said.

Rebecca gave a pig-like snort. "Doubtful."

If only Rebecca realized how Archie was right. Plenty of things were worse besides old age. Like a backstabbing friend or wondering if said friend was capable of blackmail and murder.

Deep breaths. I'd figure out how to handle Mallory—eventually, that was. The only problem was wanting to do something about my suspicions and making a plan were two different things.

Asking Gemma if she thought Mallory was vindictive enough to drive Tommy out of town or maybe even kill him was out of the question. Incest didn't quite roll off the tongue. Gemma also probably couldn't tell me anything new. Her hatred of Mallory wasn't a secret, so I needed another option. Perhaps I could try reading Mallory's diary again. There might've been entries after the one I read from June.

Damn. If only I kept reading her journal that day. If I had, I might've had more concrete answers and wouldn't have kept tapping my feet in contemplation of what would happen next.

FRIDAY, NOVEMBER 30, 2018

Archie approached me in the hallway right when I almost arrived at my locker.

I didn't count on him pulling away when I kissed him, though. Archie had never been shy about showing affection before.

"Did I do something wrong?" I asked.

"It's not you—it's me."

"Come again?"

"I don't wanna see you anymore," Archie said.

"Where's this coming from?"

"The threesome opened my eyes. Anything I feel for you doesn't change my feelings for Mallory. I've always been more interested in her."

I folded my arms. "What game is she playing? If she's making you end our relationship, then you need to tell me. Remember what we said? No more secrets."

His tongue wet his lips. "There's nothing to explain. Mallory is who I wanna be with—not you."

"What changed between our double date with Dan and Rebecca and this morning?"

"I wanted to be honest—it's what we both deserve."

Bullshit. I didn't deserve this random conversation. Threesome aside, Archie and I were enjoying our second chance.

So, yeah. Something didn't add up, and I'd discover what that fact was. It was my only option—I wouldn't be a victim. Not anymore.

SATURDAY, DECEMBER 1, 2018

I cried into my pillow while afternoon sunlight beamed into my bedroom.

No matter how much I wanted to pretend I was okay, I couldn't. The universe somehow stole Archie from me again.

Knowing I might've lost Archie again before he ended things was the worst part. Surprise was one thing—then I couldn't blame myself—yet I wasn't clueless to Mallory's antics. Archie was the fastest way to hurt me, and I shouldn't have allowed myself to become too comfortable with him.

I wouldn't feel guilty for obsessing too much over a relationship, though. Healthy or not, I always had a soft spot for Bella and Edward's romance in *Twilight*. No matter how frivolous the *Twilight* books and movies were to some, they captured the intensity from experiencing that first teen love.

Someone knocked on my door.

"May I come in?" Mom asked.

"I don't feel like talking."

"You aren't going to get anywhere if you sulk in your bedroom the entire weekend."

When Mom was right, she was right. Mom could be a sympathetic listener even if she couldn't wave a wand and fix my relationship with Archie. So maybe, just maybe, I'd save my energy for once in my life, and go with the easy solution. Doing so was the least I deserved—life shouldn't have been this difficult.

I gasped. "Fine. You can come in."

Mom entered my bedroom, then I sat up and she sat down next to me on my bed.

"I don't understand why Archie would suddenly end your relationship," Mom said.

"Because of that bitch Mallory."

"What does Mallory have to do with anything?" Mom asked.

"She wants to make my life hell."

Mom flinched. "I'm sure that isn't true—you two are best friends."

"Not anymore," I interrupted.

"I don't understand what changed?" Mom asked. "You've known Mallory your entire life."

"People put on masks sometimes."

"What do customs have to do with anything?"

No offense to Mom, but she wasn't helping the conversation. I didn't know how we'd make any progress if she couldn't infer the deeper meaning to my comment. It wasn't like I asked her to solve a math problem.

I shook my head. "It's a metaphor."

"Oh. Well, no wonder you're the writer."

"Something terrible is going on—I just don't know what it is."

Mom parted a lock of my hair to the side while several tears dripped down my face. "I've been meaning to chat with you about Archie."

I almost choked. "I don't like the sound of this."

"Relax. You aren't in trouble." She remained silent for a second. "However, there's a few things we should get straight."

"Go ahead. My life can't get any worse."

"You're too serious about Archie," Mom blurted.

"What did you just say?"

"It's not a criticism—it's a fact."

I sobbed even louder. "I'm entitled to an epic romance like everyone else."

"That's not my point."

"Then what?" I said, raising my voice.

"Enjoying the first love trope in books and television shows is one thing, but that's not real life. Your first love isn't usually your last love."

Mom should've saved her breath. I never once thought that the books or television shows I consumed were realistic—they were only escapism. I also knew what day of the week and year it was in addition to who was currently president of the United States. And if she implied what I thought she did, then we'd have big problems.

"What? Do you think I'm psychotic?" I asked.

"Don't put words in my mouth."

I rubbed my fingers against the pillow tucked under my left armpit. "Just calling it like I see it."

"Forget it." Mom stood. "I've only made things worse. Anyway, we can have whatever you want for dinner—just let me know if that means a home cooked meal or ordering takeout." Mom left my bedroom without another word, leaving me to myself.

I smacked my cheek. Mom shouldn't have been the enemy—she only tried to help—yet she could've had more sensitivity. She would've been the first person screaming bloody murder if someone told her holidays, birthdays, and anniversaries should've gotten easier by now and that any lingering grief over Dad wasted time.

SUNDAY, DECEMBER 2, 2018

I left Starbucks sometime in the early part of the afternoon.

Mom had given me thirty dollars for Starbucks and to treat myself for lunch, and I hadn't hesitated about accepting money from her. Even if some people might've thought getting money from my mother should've stopped by a certain age.

I literally bumped into Kelly several moments later after shuffling down the sidewalk. Then, she almost dropped the white box she was carrying.

I sighed. "Sorry. I should've paid attention to where I was going."

"Don't worry about it. The tiramisu will be fine."

"What's the occasion?"

Kelly giggled. "You don't need an occasion for tiramisu."

"True."

Her hair fluttered in the wind. "Are you okay, Chad?"

"I'm fine."

"You don't have to put on a façade for me. Being Mallory's sister means having my own fair share of baggage with her."

"Really?" I asked.

"She told me about how Archie ended things with you and reunited with her."

"Interesting," I mumbled.

Her eyebrows shot up. "Yeah, I didn't buy her story—not even for a second."

"I don't know what to do…"

"Fight for your happiness. Don't let Archie go."

I rubbed my eyes. "I'm sorry—I'm being a baby. You've got no reason to listen to me purge my feelings."

"Not a big deal. Always happy to listen." Kelly peeked at her gold watch. "I've gotta get going but know one thing. My door is always open at school, so don't hesitate about reaching out if you need a sympathetic ear."

"Thanks."

I didn't know if I should smile or scream. Kelly was only an acquaintance at best, yet she was more helpful than Mom. And that fact didn't comfort me—Mom was supposed to love me unconditionally no matter how neurotic I might've been. We were all that we had left in light of Dad no longer being alive.

"Don't look so sad," called out a voice.

I titled my head. Gemma just exited a nearby shop and was walking towards me. Perfect. Perhaps Gemma would also be more sympathetic than Mom.

"Why are you so happy?" I asked.

Gemma adjusted her coat's belt. "Someone I hate is about to get what's coming to them."

"Care to share?"

"Some surprises are worth it."

"I'm not sure about that anymore," I said.

She played with her ponytail. "You can vent about your boy problems if you want."

"I'm all talked out at this point."

"I'm a good listener."

Good to know I still had my intuition—I wasn't completely certainty about whether Gemma actually wanted to chat. She didn't owe me anything because we were friends or family. So, yeah. No matter how much my breakup with Archie sucked, I'd find a small amount of delight in my gut instincts remaining accurate. I didn't know what I would've done if I could no longer read situations and people.

"Let's just say you aren't the only one who still hates Mallory," I touted.

Gemma snorted. "Her karma is coming."

"Mallory was who you were referring to?"

"Yeah. Who did you think my comment was about?" Gemma asked.

"You're right. I should've known better."

Her lips spread, forming a smile. "Be patient—justice will be worth it."

"It better."

"Have a good rest of the day." Gemma trekked down the block, heading towards her Mercedes.

Yup. Morality once again didn't matter.

Gemma provided me with more comfort than she realized. Some people deserved every bad thing headed their way, and I wouldn't apologize for believing that idea. Not when Mallory wasn't an innocent victim. Nope. She'd always be a heartless bitch in my mind, and nothing changed that fact. Not even if she saved me from a burning building. Some fractures—like broken friendships—were permanent no matter how nostalgic people were for simpler times.

196

AFTER

MONDAY, MARCH 18, 2019

I scurried towards Archie—who was chatting with a guy by his locker—before first period.

Jealousy wasn't the reason for my increased pulse, though. Even if there was something about Jake's dimples that anyone would've swooned over. I was gonna fight for my relationship with Archie whether he liked it or not. I refused to be miserable when he was making too much of a big deal out of everything.

"We've got a lot to discuss," I said.

Archie glanced at Jake. "Mind giving us a moment?"

Jake nodded. "Sure."

Jake walked away, disappearing into an adjacent hallway.

"That was rude of you," Archie said.

"There's something else you don't know. I wanted to spare you, but that was a mistake."

"What? Did Tommy let you sleep with him twice?"

"Tommy's death might've been an accident, but Mallory might be a serial killer."

Archie snorted. "What drugs are you on?"

"Go ahead—ask Kelly. Mallory's previous boyfriend, Parker, died in an alleged drowning like a guy named Jordon who also would've been in our grade if he was still alive," I said. "Parker cheated on Mallory and Jordon cheated on his girlfriend, Sami—she's on the debate team with Mallory."

"Let's say for the sake of argument that you're telling your truth," Archie said. "That still doesn't change how dating me has turned you into a toxic person."

I gasped. "Are you in love with Mallory, or something?"

Yeah. My question had to have been asked no matter how difficult doing so might've been. Caring about Mallory as more than a friend was the only reasonable explanation for his vigorous defense of her.

"No. You just need to be with someone who brings out the best in you."

The warning bell rang. Then, students and teachers drifted down the hallway.

Damn. So much for fixing my relationship, because our conversation couldn't have gone worse if I tried. And I'd probably never reunite with Archie.

TUESDAY, MARCH 19, 2019

I almost opened the library door during one of my free periods when Gemma exited it.

"How's the breakup going?" Gemma asked.

"Don't pretend you care."

She grinned. "I really am sorry things blew up in your face."

"Enough about me. How are you doing?"

"You aren't the only one being gossiped about."

"What do you mean?"

Gemma looked away. "The police might've preserved my reputation but not revealing my affair with Tommy because I'm a minor. But people can't stop chatting about my father leaving my mother and I."

"Sorry to hear that."

"Don't be—it wasn't your fault."

"Still going to counseling?"

"Yeah, and it's the best decision I ever made. I'll need tools if I ever hope to recover from all the crap my father put me through."

I chuckled. "Look at you. If I didn't know better, then I'd guess you wanna become a better person."

"I do—I'm tired of the anger."

"Good for you."

"Would you wanna go to the cafeteria and work on homework?" Gemma asked. "There aren't any free tables in the library."

"Sure."

Gemma and I trudged farther and farther away from the library. Somehow, I used up all my shock. Anybody watching Gemma and I might've thought we were friends. And for a split-second, I would've believed the person. If I had to choose between Archie's scolding, Mallory's wrath, or hanging with Gemma, then I would've chosen Gemma.

WEDNESDAY, MARCH 20, 2019

I woke up from my nap several hours after arriving home from school, only to scream. Mom was at her yoga class, which meant dealing with the person sitting at the foot of my bed by myself. And it wasn't like I could call the police. Not when I had no idea what Mallory wanted.

"Good to see you," Mallory said.

"Cut the crap. You must hate me for what I did to you."

"I don't care about hurting you anymore."

"Excuse me?" I asked.

"It's true." Mallory flipped her hair over her shoulder, accentuating its greasy texture. She must not have had time to wash her hair while being on the run. "I only want one thing from you."

"And what's that?"

"Money."

"You're out of luck."

"Disappointing me isn't in your best interest. You also don't know how much money I want," she said.

I huffed. "Fine. Tell me how much money you want."

"Five hundred thousand dollars."

Mallory should've skipped the demand and checked herself in at the local sanitarium. She was out of her mind if she hoped I'd come up with all that money. I had savings from occasional guest blog articles, but nothing even close to five hundred thousand dollars.

"What are you gonna do if I don't give you the money?" I asked.

"Kill your mother."

"She didn't do anything to you."

"True. But you'd be devastated if she died."

"You'd really do that?"

"I don't have a choice," Mallory said.

Wow. If Mallory could kill Mom without blinking, then I'd never apologize for scheming with Gemma. Mom wasn't a doll—she was a real person with real feelings. And if Mallory wanted to hurt me, then she could date Archie. She already had plenty of practice with that and using Archie to hurt me would easier than riding a bicycle.

"Meet me at Wesley Bridge at 5 p.m. on Monday," Mallory said.

"Are you forgetting what happened the last time someone demanded money?" I asked.

"You wouldn't kill me—you don't have it in you. Also, what happened to Tommy was an accident."

I stared her down. "I'd be careful. Being in cahoots with Gemma proves I'm capable of everything."

THURSDAY, MARCH 21, 2019

I approached Kelly right when she was about to walk into her office during one of my free periods.

"You're gonna wanna hear what I have to say," I said.

Kelly grunted. "Fine. You have two minutes."

I did a quick glance around the hallway. Phew. Nobody was walking by at the moment, so I didn't have to worry about someone overhearing our conversation.

"I heard from your sister yesterday," I revealed.

Kelly wiggled her eyebrows. "Oh, yeah? What did she want?"

"Five hundred thousand dollars—she's gonna leave town if she doesn't get what she wants."

"Good for her."

"She threatened to kill my mother if I didn't give her the money," I snapped, pulse pounding in my ears.

"I'm staying out of it."

"My mother doesn't deserve to die."

"Maybe not," Kelly said. "But nothing good comes from you and your friends. Mallory was remanded to my custody, which meant the cops giving me grief when she didn't turn herself in."

"Blame Archie. He opened his big mouth."

"I'm done." Kelly grabbed her key, then it clinked in the lock. She then slammed the door shut behind her, locking it.

Hating me was understandable, yet Kelly could've feigned interest in our conversation. Mallory was still her sister. She also wouldn't be getting the inheritance if it wasn't for me, so there was no need for her bitchiness. I also wasn't someone to mess with as a result of my scheming with Gemma. If Kelly became too much of a problem, then I wouldn't have given a second thought to dealing with her like I had Mallory.

FRIDAY, MARCH 22, 2019

"I can't believe you aren't gonna help me," I said.

Archie, Rebecca, Dan, and I stood in an empty hallway before first period—although not by their choice. My all capital letters group text was the only reason for them hovering in front of me right now.

Rebecca's teeth nipped her lip. "We've made up our mind."

I looked into Dan's eyes.

"I'm with Rebecca," Dan said.

"Mallory threatened to kill my mother if I can't come up with the money," I said.

"I'm sorry, but we can't have anything to do with you. Not after you went behind our backs and schemed with Gemma," Rebecca said.

"What would you do if Mallory threatened your relationship with Dan?" I asked.

"Doesn't matter. What you did was wrong. What if your scheme blew up in your face?" Rebecca asked. "There could've been consequences for Archie, Dan, and me."

I stomped my feet. "You've got no right to judge me."

"I'll spell it out for you since Rebecca and Dan are too polite," Archie said. "We don't want anything to do with you."

I fought back tears. Rebecca, Dan, and Archie wouldn't take away my courage after everything I had been through. So, I'd put on a front. Rebecca, Dan, and Archie needed a serious dose of reality.

"You're making a big mistake," I said.

"Doesn't matter—go to the police if you're that concerned about your mother. Anyway, let's go," Rebecca said to Dan and Archie.

The three of them left without another word and I wailed when they were out of earshot. Kelly's lack of cooperation was one thing, yet Dan and Rebecca were supposed to be my friends. They were supposed to do anything for me just like I would for them. Judging me was also easier when they weren't the one forced with making the difficult decisions.

Fuck. I really was alone, so I might've had to go to Detectives Garrison and Jones. I had nothing left to lose, and some help was better than no help. It wasn't like Mallory said she'd kill Mom if I went to the police.

MONDAY, MARCH 25, 2019

The blue grew thinner and thinner in the afternoon sky while I approached Wesley Bridge. Someone sporting a black, hooded sweatshirt sat on a rock by the lake, rising within seconds of my arrival.

The person yanked their hood off—it was Mallory, like I suspected. Being incognito in this moment was probably the only smart thing she'd ever done in her life.

She pursed her lips. "I don't see a briefcase."

"Yeah. You're right."

"Did you give me the money in another way—like a secret offshore account?"

Yeah. Mallory was in greater need of professional help than I realized. Running away with a more than generous nest-egg wasn't going to happen no matter how much she wished it might've.

"I don't have the money," I said.

She grunted. "Excuse me?"

"Game over, Mallory." I whistled and my throat tightened.

Detectives Garrison and Jones popped out of nearby bushes; guns drawn. "Police! Hands up!" Detective Garrison exclaimed.

Mallory put her hands up. Then, Detective Garrison shoved her hands behind her back. The handcuffs clinked while Detective Jones's gun remained drawn.

"Add attempted murder to the charges since she threatened to kill my mother," I said.

"You won't get away with this," Mallory said.

I smirked. "Watch me."

Detectives Garrison and Jones dragged Mallory towards the unmarked cop car in the distance while the glee oozing from me increased with each passing moment. Maybe, just maybe, Mallory was finally out of my life for good. I could hope, at least.

204

BEFORE

MONDAY, DECEMBER 3, 2018

I sat across from Dan and Rebecca at a booth in back of Café Tomorrow.

It was a little past noon, and we hadn't stopped surveying the menu. I couldn't account for Dan and Rebecca, yet I had a good reason for not making eye contact. Somehow, I still prayed my breakup with Archie was a nightmare I'd soon wakeup from. No matter how many times I exaggerated in the past, nothing stunk more than not having control of my life. I deserved more than going through life like a zombie.

"Anyone know what they wanna order?" Dan asked.

"Maybe a grilled cheese and tomato soup—it's a good day for it," Rebecca said. "Although perhaps I should just be thankful for having the day off."

Dan chuckled. "That's the opposite of my dad. He believes professional development days are a waste of time."

My eyes remained on the menu.

Rebecca snickered. "What? No comment?"

"I'm thankful you invited me, but I'm a third wheel," I said.

"Don't be ridiculous," Dan said. "We have plenty of alone time and are happy to spend the afternoon with you."

I rested a hand under my chin. "Please. I'm not oblivious to how I'm a burden."

Rebecca gave me a mock frown. "Don't you dare say that."

"It's true. Archie and Mallory screwed me over again," I said.

Rebecca sipped her diet soda before speaking. "My advice from almost three months ago still applies."

"And what's that?" I demanded.

"If you're this upset about Archie, then talk to him. Especially if you think he isn't telling the truth," Rebecca said.

Dan nodded. "She's right. You've gotta fight for your happiness—anyone would be lucky to date you."

"Thanks," I croaked.

"I'm serious," Rebecca said. "And I wanna hear your plan for dealing with Archie and Mallory before we finish lunch."

I chewed on the inside of my lip. Dan and Rebecca were right despite their overbearing personalities. I wouldn't change my situation with Archie if I sat on my ass. But wanting to do something and actually doing it were two different things. Especially when this wasn't my first instance of drama with Archie.

The waitress shuffled to our table. "Do you know what you wanna order?" she asked.

"Could we have another couple of minutes?" Rebecca asked.

"Sure." The waitress dashed to a table on the opposite side of the café.

"I don't buy that he still cares about Mallory." I rolled my eyes. "Please. Does Archie think I'm stupid?"

Dan flipped to the next page. "All the more reason to chat with him, man."

"I'm sorry. I must seem pathetic for always worrying about a guy," I said.

Rebecca smacked me with her menu. "I never want you to apologize for anything again. Do you understand me?"

"It'd just be nice if Mallory would go to boarding school in California or maybe on a cruise to the North Pole," I said.

Dan snorted, and soda spilled out of nose. "As if life is that easy."

"It'd be nice if it could be," I said.

Rebecca picked one of her nails. "This isn't a Disney movie."

"I don't even know what to say to Archie," I said.

"Whatever you do, don't be confrontational." Rebecca grabbed a napkin from the metal dispenser to the left of her, then blew her nose. "That's gonna push him further away, and you'll get more pissed off."

Dan almost smirked yet stopped himself by biting his lip. "Listen to her, Chad. I'd be irritated if I messed up and someone got confrontational with me."

Rebecca gave Dan a look. "Is there something I should know?"

"I was trying to make a point, babe," Dan said.

Babe. I couldn't deny how the word had a nice ring to it—I would've given anything for Archie to call me that.

Whatever. At least Dan and Rebecca were happy, because I wasn't in denial. If I couldn't be content, then my best friends enjoying themselves was the next best thing. Dan and Rebecca's relationship also reinforced the saying about how the more things change, the more they stay the same. In my case, that meant Dan and Rebecca always being there for me. I couldn't fathom how people dealt with shit all by themselves.

Outside trees bobbed after a gust of wind swooshed down the block, and my stomach lurched.

The numerous thoughts swirling in my mind weren't about the impending cold weather, though. Archie and Mallory just darted by Café Tomorrow. But spending time together wasn't enough for them. Nope. They were also holding hands.

And for a split-second, I gave into the negativity and dug my nails into my palms. I should've been holding hands with Archie, not Mallory.

So, yeah. No matter how challenging talking with Archie would be, I didn't have a choice. Besides, the conversation couldn't be as bad as our breakup—nothing surpassed how I would've rather been gutted like a fish then have my budding romance with Archie end.

WEDNESDAY, DECEMBER 5, 2018

Time to chat with Archie.

Putting off our conversation yesterday was bad enough—every day I didn't tell Archie how I felt was another day he grew closer to Mallory. So, I approached him in the school hallway before first period when he was about to open his locker.

"We need to talk," I said.

He averted his gaze. "I have nothing to say to you."

"If you're gonna lie, then you should have more confidence."

"I'm not hiding anything."

"I know there's more to the story, and I deserve to know the truth."

"I don't owe you anything," Archie said.

I whimpered. "If you ever cared about me, then you'll be honest."

"I don't have time for this." Archie tried walking away from me, yet I cut him off. He wasn't getting away. Not that easily. Not when I wasn't any closer to finding out the truth about his recent behavior change.

"If Mallory is in trouble, then tell me," I said.

Yup. Just because I knew about Tommy's empty trust fund, the argument he had with Mallory the day after the Fourth of July, Mallory finding out Gemma and Tommy, and Mallory's missing tape, didn't mean I had to reveal everything all at once to Archie. I didn't know what Archie knew, so I'd take the cautious approach for now.

"There's nothing to reveal," he said. "Mallory is the one I'm interested in, not you."

"You don't mean that."

His eyes lit up. "I do. You were just something to pass the time, and I'm bored now."

"Don't bullshit me."

"It's not my fault you're too wrapped up in your own delusions to see reality," Archie said.

Deep breaths. I could cry later in the bathroom stall or when I got home. No need for Archie to see me get worked up. No thanks. Preserving my pride was the least I was entitled to—vulnerability was a weakness I couldn't afford.

"I thought the indecent proposal was the worst thing that could happen to me, but I was wrong," I said.

"Accept the truth. We're done, and no amount of conversations or gestures will change that," Archie said.

The bell rang.

"And now I'm gonna be late for first period because of you." Archie smacked his shoulder against mine, then headed to his locker.

Good to know Archie was Mr. Sensitive. Arriving to first period should've been the least of his concerns if he ever loved me. But no. So, the only question was if I had the guts to fight for my happiness or if I'd continue stewing in my contempt.

THURSDAY, DECEMBER 6, 2018

I meandered through the hallway on the way to lunch, only to cross paths with Archie and Mallory. And they weren't only spending time together or holding hands like on Monday when I was at Café Tomorrow with Dan and Rebecca. They were currently engaged in a PDA, and I almost vomited. Mallory didn't deserve to be happy—not for a second. Not after everything she did to me.

I coughed. "We're at school."

Archie and Mallory pulled back from each other.

Archie's cheeks flushed. "We didn't see you there, Chad."

"Yeah, we did," Mallory said. "We just didn't care."

I scoffed. "We're you always this cruel?"

Mallory squeezed Archie's hand. "It's not cruel to be with the person I'm meant to be with."

"I'm not buying your story, not even for a second," I said.

"Doesn't matter what you think," Mallory said. "Now that Archie isn't with you, we can finally be together."

I shifted my posture, then a poster on the wall behind me caught my attention from the corner of my eye. But no amount of fancy fonts tempted me into going to the dance. Not when I didn't have anyone to go with.

"Tell me something. Are you going to the Snowflake Ball tomorrow?" I asked.

"Nope," Mallory interrupted. "We're gonna go my house right after school tomorrow and have a movie marathon"

"Sounds fishy. You guys should wanna make your big debut," I said.

Mallory grabbed Archie's hand for the millionth time. "We don't have to prove anything to anyone."

"What Mallory said," Archie murmured.

"You might wanna give your boyfriend a lesson on public speaking," I said.

"We don't have to stand here and take this." Mallory gripped Archie by the arm, then darted down the hallway.

I hollered at them, though. They weren't getting away that easily. And fortunately for me, they turned around.

Mallory grunted. "What now?"

"One way or another, I'm gonna discover what's going on," I said. "You might think you've won, but you're wrong. People talk and your personal business isn't as private as you might think."

Yup. I wouldn't miss an opportunity to twist the knife about Tommy's disappearance. Sometimes, the best victories were subtle.

"Whatever," Mallory said before darting out of sight with Archie.

I could sob now that Archie and Mallory were out of sight—nobody else happened to be walking down the hallway either. No matter how many times I contemplated everything that happened since the beginning of the school year, I couldn't fathom how my life became so complicated. And I'd pray my life would return to normal soon—even if that meant confronting Archie and Mallory again tomorrow after school. There was something about Mallory's response to the Snowflake Ball that left a bitter feeling in my mouth.

212

AFTER

WEDNESDAY, MARCH 27, 2019

Archie approached me before first period in the high school parking lot right after I exited my car.

He smiled. "Is your mother okay?"

"Don't pretend to care about her or me. You should be ashamed of yourself after how you, Rebecca, and Dan iced me out."

His face drooped. "You're right. That was harsh."

"I didn't deserve that." Tears welled in my eyes. After a little more than two and half years, I could no longer filter my feelings. Archie hadn't been the love of my life, yet I'd be lying if I didn't admit being curious about whether we could have a real relationship if the circumstances had been different. I was his friend, and he owed me a conversation if he didn't wanna continue our friendship.

"I'm not trying to upset you," Archie said.

"Too late."

Wind ripped through the air, but it lacked its usual vindictive coldness. Perhaps spring was actually here, and winter would be a distant memory.

"I can't imagine how messed up you must be from Tommy and I'm willing to give you another chance."

"How big of you."

"Fine. I deserved that."

"I'm thankful you're willing to give me another chance, but I can't be with someone who'll bail on a moment's notice."

"But I'm sorry."

"That doesn't change what happened. And our relationship also might not be meant to be—it shouldn't be difficult."

"That's bullshit," Archie said.

Tears fell down my cheeks. "You judged me, and now you've gotta live with your choice."

He put his hands on his hips. "What? You wanna punish me just like you did Mallory?"

"My reasoning is about protecting myself, not punishing. Goodbye, Archie." I scurried away from Archie, yet I waited till I approached the high school's front entrance before sobbing.

I had to stand by my decision no matter how difficult it was. It took me a long time to realize the truth, but Archie didn't ensure stability. Drama always existed—whether he started it, or Mallory did.

So, yeah. Archie and I were finished.

THURSDAY, MARCH 28, 2019

I continued staring at my plate—which contained two slices of pizza—while Mom and I sat at the dining room table.

She giggled. "Aren't you hungry."

"I can't do this." I rose.

"I wasn't kidding about eating more dinners together. You worked with the police to apprehend a fugitive without telling me, and I can't just pretend that didn't happen."

I shrieked. "Great. Maybe you and Archie can start a club—you both love punishing me."

"This isn't about discipline, it's about you being my son. I'd be devastated if something happened to you."

"You don't need to know everything going on in my life," I said.

"Says who?"

I made a fist. "Mallory threatened to kill you, Mom."

"All the more reason to loop me in."

"The police knowing was enough."

"I don't wanna fight." Mom bit into her pizza. "Nothing you say can push me away from you."

"You've got no idea what my life is like," I said, speaking louder.

"Then tell me."

My stomach churned. "I didn't lose my virginity to Archie—I lost it to Tommy. He asked me to sleep with him before he cut me out of his life the start of freshman year."

Mom didn't respond.

"And he might've possibly liked me, but I'll never know," I said. "I thought I was doing him a favor in addition to how it felt so good for him to want me. But I was wrong."

Mom once again didn't say anything. Instead, she stood and hugged me. I didn't push her away, though. Not this time. A simple thing was the only thing I had to hold onto, and I'd take it. I just wasn't sure what I was supposed to do with my life at this point. Not when I didn't have anything to look forward to.

FRIDAY, MARCH 29, 2019

"I'm surprised you wanted my company," I said.

Rebecca and I stood in back of Anna's Chocolate Shop after school, going through the various selections of chocolate and other candies. Apparently, Rebecca needed help with picking out a gift for Dan's upcoming birthday.

"I should apologize. Everyone makes mistakes, and I shouldn't have judged you so harshly about scheming with Gemma. You did what you felt was best," Rebecca said.

"How kind of you."

Rebecca glared. "I'm trying to make amends."

"Fine. I forgive you."

"I should also be thanking you for something."

"And what's that?" I asked.

"I know you helped Dan pick out the dress for our anniversary."

I removed my gaze from the chocolates, focusing on Rebecca now. "So?"

"Dan and I know you're a good person and are proud to call you our friend."

"Thanks."

Rebecca locked her arms. "But I could kick your ass for not forgiving Archie. He told me about how he tried making amends with you."

"I don't wanna talk about it."

The shop's bell chimed, and several kids dashed into the shop, almost knocking over a few boxes of chocolate on a table by the front door.

"Be careful not to spend too much money," said a woman who remained by the shop's entrance.

Rebecca leaned closer. "If you want to be happy, then don't let your pride get in the way. You don't get unlimited chances in life. Also, Mallory isn't a threat."

"She's still in town."

"Locked away at Wren Sanitarium," Rebecca interrupted.

"I'll think about it."

She giggled. "I've got faith you'll make the right decision."

Admitting Rebecca was right pained me less than it should've. I couldn't argue with her because she wasn't wrong. If I didn't wanna be with Archie, then fine. But I had to make sure I could live with my decision. Having Archie be the next Tommy—wondering what could've been, five years from now—was the last thing I wanted or needed.

So maybe, just maybe, I'd forgive Archie one day—just not today. Hanging with Rebecca was a callback to simpler times, and I wouldn't trade this moment for anything in the word.

SUNDAY, MARCH 31, 2019

Rain pattered against the grass while I stood in front of Dad's grave.

"Being in a cemetery is kind of morbid even for you," called out a voice.

I titled my head. "It's the anniversary of my father's death."

"I know."

"What are you doing here?" I asked.

Archie's grip on his umbrella tightened while wind swished through the cemetery as he shuffled towards me.

"I stopped by your house and your mother told me you were here," he revealed.

"I'm not into the mood to rehash everything."

"Good. I don't wanna fight."

"Then what?" I demanded.

"I don't know how else to make it up to you, but I'm sorry for judging you too harshly," Archie said.

"And why should I believe you?"

"I'd die if anything happened to you. Contrary to what you might believe, meeting you is one of the best things that ever happened to me."

"Mallory is gonna be released from the sanitarium one day," I forced out.

"Let that be tomorrow's problem."

Rain slammed into the ground—even louder and faster than when I first arrived—while I stole a glance at Archie. There was no guarantee that my life would be perfect with Archie, yet there was no harm in trying to make our relationship work, because I might've been wrong about my previous thought. If something was difficult, then that didn't mean it wasn't worth having—I just had to fight harder. Nothing came easily in life, including relationships. So, yeah. Archie deserved another chance.

"I forgive you," I said.

Archie closed his umbrella, then placed it on the ground. He kissed me while more wind whipped through the air and his umbrella flew away. He didn't chase after it. Instead, his soft lips pressed against my mouth and goosebumps spread over my arms and legs. We'd enjoy this moment, weather be damned.

MONDAY, APRIL 1, 2019

Archie and I walked through the school hallway before first period, holding hands.

Rebecca and Dan—who stood by Dan's locker—by smiled at us.

"What do we have here?" Rebecca asked.

"We worked things out," I said.

Dan nodded. "We can tell."

"About damn time," Rebecca said.

"If this is what happiness resembles, then I never want this feeling to end," I said.

"Good to know you care about me," Archie said.

Archie should've known better than to say what he just had. I absolutely cared about him and nothing anyone did changed that fact. All of our mistakes remained in the past. Visiting Mallory at some point might've helped, though. Something to let her know I'd always be in control—especially since there were still facts she didn't know about. Facts even Rebecca, Dan, and Archie weren't privy too. But that was fine. Full disclosure wasn't required for my friendship with Rebecca and Dan or for dating Archie. Although whether seeing Mallory one last time was a good idea remained to be seen. Gloating was one thing, yet

I couldn't forget about hubris after all the times my English teachers drummed that theme into my head.

"Let's hope Mallory never returns," Dan said.

Rebecca gave Dan a mock frown. "Please!"

"It had to be said," Dan said.

"Let's not think about Mallory," I said.

Archie let go of my hand, adjusting his backpack strap. "Sounds like a plan."

TUESDAY, APRIL 2, 2019

Dan, Rebecca, Archie, and I sat at a table in the middle of the cafeteria while various bounced against the walls.

"I could kick myself—I can't believe I haven't taken the SAT's yet," Rebecca said.

"That makes two of us," Dan said.

Archie took another bite of his sandwich. "Me three."

"Me four," I said.

Rebecca whipped her head back and forth. "We're never going to get into college let alone finish high school with this attitude."

"There's still time," I said.

"Let's not fart around." Rebecca finished her Gatorade, then tossed it into an adjacent garbage can.

Dan wagged his finger at his girlfriend. "You worry too much."

"Our futures are important," Rebecca said.

Archie laughed. "I'm fine with working at McDonald's."

"Speak for yourself," Rebecca said.

Appreciating the less serious moments once again couldn't be avoided. Polite bickering what was my life should've been like at the beginning of the school year, not speculating about Mallory's next betrayal or if we'd go to jail for being accomplishes.

Footsteps sounded, and I looked up. Gemma just clipped by our table.

"Gemma," I said.

She halted. "How are you Chad?"

"Fine. What about you?" I asked.

"I'm good—just worried about the SAT's," Gemma said, hands remaining on her lunch tray.

"What a coincidence. We were just having a conversation about that," I said.

Gemma's eyebrows inched up. "Really?"

"Yeah. Anyway, are you eating lunch with anyone?" I asked.

"I was just gonna have my lunch quickly and then head to the library," Gemma said.

"Would you like to join us?" I asked.

Rebecca leaned into my right ear. "What are you doing?"

"We'd love your company," I said, ignoring Rebecca.

"Sure. Company would be great." Gemma sat down between Rebecca and Dan before Rebecca gave me a brief dirty look.

Too bad for Rebecca, but I wouldn't change my opinion. Nothing bad would happen from eating lunch with Gemma. She didn't have any contagious diseases, and we'd all be better people for including her at lunch. I didn't know everything, yet I didn't have to in order to appreciate how Gemma must've had a difficult life in light of her father and losing Tommy. Both Mallory and Tommy also might've been different people if someone showed them real kindness. A few seconds of speculation was all that was needed for pondering if Gemma would be the next to snap.

"Do you know when you're gonna take the SAT's?" Dan asked.

"In June." Gemma scarfed down a bite of her salad. "But I'm more concerned about AP Exams next month.

Rebecca clapped her hand against her cheek. "Fuck. I forgot about those."

"Relax, there's still plenty of time to prepare," Gemma said.

WEDNESDAY, APRIL 3, 3019

I sat at a table in the back of Starbucks, and someone joined me several minutes after my arrival, so looked up. I wasn't expecting company yet had a suspicion about who it was based on the high-pitched giggle.

"What do you want, Andrea?" I asked.

"No need to be curt."

"I'm impressed. You know a big word."

"I saw you and just thought I'd say hello." She ran her fingers through her hair, accentuating her bob. Wow. Perhaps I wasn't the only one who needed a radical change. Her hair extended several inches past her shoulders last time I checked. Although she still had pink streaks, which deserved kudos no matter how much I cringed in her presence. Most people wouldn't have had the guts to do something like that in our town. People looked at anyone who was different with the same contempt they would've given a five-eyed person.

She snickered. "What a shocker. You don't have anything to say."

"I don't wanna fight."

"This might be hard to believe, but I don't wanna start trouble."

"We don't have to be polite with each other. The world will survive if we aren't friends." I sipped my iced caramel macchiato, extra caramel on top jolting my taste buds.

"I disagree."

"Get to your point."

She shifted her posture in her chair. "You reunited with Archie."

"So? Determined to make another play for me?"

"Don't flatter yourself."

"You haven't done anything to give me a positive impression of you."

"I'm a flirt; not a genuine threat."

"Whatever," I said.

"For what it's worth, I'm glad you and Archie solved your problems."

I chuckled. "No offense but I don't need your approval. I had no doubt that Archie and I would reunite."

"That's not what Archie said."

"This is my way of extending friendship." Andrea offered her hand, yet I didn't take it. She might've been pulling me in for a kiss, and I couldn't have that. Not when I would've died if the universe robbed me of my future with Archie again. Some people didn't change who they were no matter how much they believed their lie.

"Wonderful."

Not wishing anyone but Mallory bad didn't mean I had to sit here and take Andrea's commentary. Andrea should've known a lost cause when she saw one. I deserved to look out for myself because of everything Mallory did to me. I challenged anyone not to eat and breathe skepticism 24/7 after dealing with a toxic best friend. Words could only go far, and sometimes real action was required. Even if doing so entailed pushing people away. Under different circumstances—like if she wasn't flirtatious or I hadn't dealt with Mallory—Andrea and I might've been friends. Her quirkiness would've provided endless fodder for my writing, because I needed no help with imagining the trouble we'd get into if we became friends.

"I have a boyfriend now," Andrea said.

"What happened to making a splash?"

"My parents are still pissed about boarding school."

I scowled. "Can you blame them?"

"If I wanted a lecture, then I wouldn't tune out my parents." She offered her hand for a second time. "What do you say? Friends?"

I didn't respond. Instead, my grip tightened on my beverage.

"You can never have enough allies," Andrea continued. "Not when Mallory will be released one day."

"What do you know about Mallory?"

"I pay attention to gossip from Archie and my parents."

I shook her hand. "Okay. I can live with that."

Yeah. I wasn't lying—not this time. I couldn't boost Andrea's ego, yet she made a good point. Mallory would rejoin society one day no matter how preferable denial was. And that would be fantastic. No telling what she'd do to me after everything I did to her. If there was one guarantee in life, it was the cyclical nature of revenge. She hurt me, I hurt her, then rinse and repeat—our game of psychological warfare resembling a carousel that never stopped spinning.

"I should also thank you," Andrea said.

"Feeling okay? That's the last thing I'd expect from you."

Andrea jabbed my shoulder. "Quit it. We're gonna be friends, and you can't do anything about that fact."

"You were saying?" I interrupted.

"Right." She licked her lips. "I'm glad you didn't involve Archie with your meetup with Mallory."

"And why is that?"

"I'd die if anything happened to him. We're always there for each other no matter how turbulent our dynamic has been."

"Really?" I slurped the rest of my beverage.

"Yeah, I'd die if anything happened to him."

"No need for theatrics."

"It's the truth—family is everything—whether you believe it or not."

Wow. Life would always be filled with surprises. I never once expected Andrea to care about anything but herself. So, I wouldn't cut her out for interrupting my alone time. Discovering her humanity meant having one less problem. I didn't know what I would've done if the Mallory debacle ended only for another to begin. Doubt wasn't that difficult to manipulate—the power of suggestion caused more problems than physical violence could.

"I'll go order my drink now," Andrea said.

"Great."

So, yeah. Andrea and I would give this friendship thing a try. If our dynamic changed, then I could always change my mind.

BEFORE

FRIDAY, DECEMBER 7, 2018

I rang Mallory's doorbell.

No matter how difficult my mission was, I had to do it. I wasn't gonna lose Archie to Mallory for a third time. To hell with worrying about seeming frivolous because of arguing over a guy. Archie provided me happiness—the kind of joy I would've gotten from having multiple snow days in a row—and I'd hold onto it.

If getting Archie back entailed an unpleasant conversation with him and Mallory, then so be it. Her con was up, and there was nothing Mallory could do about it. Not even if she stomped her feet against the ground and threw a million tantrums. There was no spinning Tommy's missing trust fund money, the argument Tommy's lake house neighbor witnessed between Mallory and Tommy the day after the Fourth of July, Mallory's diary entry about finding Tommy in bed with Gemma, the missing video, and Archie ending our relationship only to start following Mallory around like a guard dog.

I pressed Mallory's doorbell for a second time.

No answer.

The wind rattled against Mallory's house so loudly that someone might as well have screamed. I shivered before stuffing my hands into my jacket pockets.

Mallory and Archie were gonna have to try harder if they wanted to me leave. Especially since the living room light remained on.

Fuck it. Maybe knocking on the door several times was my answer, so that was what I did.

In addition to getting answers from Archie and Mallory, it would've been nice for them to let me inside since the blue almost completely waned from the afternoon sky. Standing outside in the dark was the last thing I wanted to do on a Friday evening.

Damn. Still no answer.

Time to make another fist and bang on the front door. I had nothing to lose—it wasn't like the neighbors called the cops on me.

The door opened, revealing Mallory.

She hissed. "What are you doing here?"

"We need to talk, and I'm not taking no for an answer."

"This isn't a good time," Mallory spat. "And if you ever cared about our friendship, you'll leave."

"Guilt trips don't work on me," I said.

Her eye bulged. "I'm serious, Chad. You've gotta get out of here. You have no idea what's going on."

"Then tell me."

"I'm doing you a favor by demanding you leave," she said.

Please. Mallory should've known better than to insult my intelligence. I was a teenager, not a preschooler.

"Please. You're just trying to steal Archie from me again," I said. "Well, sorry, but it's not gonna work."

Footsteps squeaked against the wooden floor. A guy stood next to Mallory.

"I'm not a toy," Archie said.

No need for Archie to state the obvious. The awkwardness of my response didn't change its truthfulness. Mallory took Archie from me for a third time, and I wouldn't let her succeed. This was real life, not an indie movie where criminals never suffered consequences.

"If you don't let me inside, then I'm gonna scream," I bellowed.

Mallory grunted. "You're too much."

"Just let him in—he's not gonna leave," Archie said.

"Fine. Have it your way." Mallory yanked me inside, then closed the front door behind her. In fact, she couldn't haven't shut the door any faster if she tried. If I didn't know better, then I would've thought she made a deal with the Devil and he was about to collect.

We shuffled into the living room.

My nostrils flared. "I know what's going on, Mallory. Like with how Tommy cheated on you with Gemma. What I can't figure out was if you blackmailed him to leave town and he did, or if you went further and killed him."

Mallory crossed her arms. "Thinking you know everything must be nice. But as usual, you have no idea what you're talking about."

"Don't be so harsh," Archie said.

"Quit defending him," Mallory quipped.

I bit my lip. "I wanna know why Archie broke up with me."

"You're right," Mallory revealed. "I blackmailed Tommy to leave town because of my tape I made of him and Gemma."

Archie massaged his forehead. "But Tommy recently came back to town. He blew through his trust fund and wants more money to stay silent—five million dollars to be exact."

"Archie and I also think he's the one who stole the flash drive—the one with the video of him and Gemma," Mallory said.

"I don't understand," I said.

"That's why you can't be here," Mallory said, struggling to catch a breath. "He's gonna arrive any minute."

I laughed. "Wow. You actually sound scared."

"This isn't funny." Mallory pushed her sleeve up. "He did this to me."

My eyes remained glued to Mallory's left arm. More specifically, her black and blue coated wrist. Wow. Hard to picture Mallory as the victim after everything she did to me.

I didn't have to be psychic to believe Mallory wasn't faking her feelings. It wasn't like she was a special effects makeup artist, skilled in prosthetics. Plus asking Archie to hit her just for show didn't seem likely either.

"Let me guess. You don't have the money," I said.

Archie hung his head. "You should go. I'll call you tomorrow when this is all over."

Tears welled in my eyes. "Why end things with me?"

"Isn't it obvious?" Mallory demanded. "Tommy is a threat, and it'd help to have a fake boyfriend."

"Even if it meant hurting me?" I asked.

"That wasn't my intention—not this time," Mallory said.

"I don't believe you. Not anymore," I said.

"It doesn't matter what you believe. You're leaving." Mallory grabbed my arm, then dragged me through the living room and to the front door. Except the front door just slammed shut.

"Nobody is going anywhere," said a voice.

The three of us turned around. A guy with combed-back black hair stood by the front door.

Mallory glanced at the metal object in Tommy's right hand, then made eye contact with him. "Let Chad go. He isn't part of this."

"He is now," Tommy said. "Besides, he'd go to the police."

"I wouldn't," I said, voice quaking.

Tommy waved the gun at me. "I've got no reason to believe you, Chad. We haven't been friends for a long time."

"And whose fault is that?" I asked.

"You're right—mistreating you is the one thing I regret. Too bad things didn't turn out differently after that summer afternoon," Tommy said, placing his left hand over his right, which remained on the gun.

"What are you saying?" I asked.

Tommy scoffed. "Isn't it obvious?"

If I didn't know any better, I would've thought Tommy just implied he had a crush on me. But that possibility didn't matter. Not when he could fire bullets at a moment's notice, because I would've been in denial if I didn't acknowledge my increased pulse.

"Why do you have the gun pointed at me?" I asked. "I didn't blackmail you."

"You make good leverage until I get my money," Tommy said.

Mallory shook her head. "Sorry to ruin your plans, but I don't have the money."

"That's a shame. I was counting on leaving town tonight, because I wouldn't be alone this time," Tommy said.

Archie's brow lifted. "What? Are you leaving town with Gemma?"

"That's for me to know and for you to find out," Tommy said. "But if you really don't have the money, then I should just kill Chad."

Mallory grumbled at Tommy. "I bet you stole the flash drive from my bedroom."

"Yes, I did," Tommy said, smirk expanding. "You should've known better than to leave your spare key under the doormat."

Mallory tossed her hair over her shoulders. "You're unbelievable."

"Sometimes I forget how clueless you are," Tommy said. "If I was gonna extort money from you, then I had to make sure you didn't have any leverage."

"Where's the flash drive now?" Mallory asked.

Tommy cackled. "Someplace safe."

I smacked my hands together. "Please, Tommy. You don't have to murder me."

"It's not like I wanna kill you. Mallory just needs to know actions have consequences." His tongue wet his lips. "Any last words?"

Fuck. Tommy was gonna shoot me, and I couldn't do a damn thing about it. And that fact was just great. Robbing me of my entire future might've been the universe's greatest sin against me.

"Just do it," I mumbled.

"Things could've been so different," Tommy said, hands still wrapped around the gun.

"Go to Hell!" Mallory grabbed the bookend on the mahogany table in front of us, then smacked it against Tommy's head.

Tommy collapsed onto his back after teetering backwards. The gun clanked against the floor, yet by some miracle, it didn't go off. Blood trickled from Tommy's forehead, splattering onto his shirt and staining it red.

"Come here, Chad." Archie opened his arms, inviting me in for a hug.

Regardless of our relationship status, I fell into his chest with the same grace of a ballet dancer preforming a recital. Archie continued patting my back. I even sobbed while my head remained buried in his shirt. This evening was the closest I'd ever come to dying, and it couldn't happen again. No matter how irksome the universe was, I deserved to live my life.

I couldn't forget about another fact, though—Mallory saved my life. I didn't know what I would've done if she hadn't hit Tommy in the head with a bookend. And as much as I wanted to blame Archie for remaining frozen, I couldn't. I would've done the same thing as him. Doing nothing was sometimes the easiest thing.

AFTER

THURSDAY, APRIL 4, 2019

A humid breeze trickled through the air while the moon's glow provided extra lighting. I shuffled to the end of my driveway while crickets chirped from a nearby pond. Then, I got into the car parked by the curb.

I cocked my head. "This couldn't have waited till morning?"

Kelly bit her nail. "We can't have this conversation at school."

"Doesn't mean this clandestine meeting is any less creepy."

"You'll get over it."

"What do you want?" I asked.

"I can't do this anymore. We need to find a way for Mallory to be released from the sanitarium without implicating ourselves."

"It's too late for buyer's remorse."

Kelly sneered. "Mallory is the only family I have."

"You weren't thinking about that when you inherited your parents' money."

"I was wrong—there's more to life than being rich."

"We're not changing the plan—not now. I worked too hard for my happy ending with Archie, and your conscience isn't gonna ruin everything."

"How can you be so cold?" she asked.

Kelly needed a reality check ASAP—she couldn't have said what she had. Nothing could ruin my now perfect life, and I'd repeat that sentiment as much as I needed to. I deserved a happy ending after all the crap that occurred since the beginning of the school year, and I wouldn't let anyone tell me otherwise. Judging me was also much easier when Kelly hadn't dealt with half the stuff I had.

I rolled my eyes. "Have you forgotten everything your sister did to me? Like her indecent proposal scheme last fall?"

"That's in the past," Kelly said.

"People don't change. I believe a person once they show me who they are," I said.

"That's harsh." Kelly paused for a beat. "Have you forgotten how Mallory saved your life?"

I chuckled. "We both know that isn't the whole story."

"What are you talking about?" Kelly removed her leather jacket and placed it on her lap. After that, she scowled. "Don't tell me you're so delusional that you can't acknowledge how Mallory saved your life?"

"That's only partially true, because there's something you don't realize," I said.

"And what's that?"

"I saw everything." I pressed my head against the front passenger window while an animal howled. Hopefully, it wasn't a coyote attacking a deer. I cringed just from imagining a coyote's teeth ripping apart the deer's flesh, making blood spill everywhere. Kind of like my current emotional state from the direction our conversation would soon take. There was no undoing my revelation once I dropped it.

Kelly snorted. "I should've known you were making an empty threat."

"Hardly."

My head remained against the car window while my mind drifted back to the Snowflake Ball. More specifically, what happened after Mallory smacked Tommy in the head with a bookend. Mallory didn't realize I knew something she didn't, and that was worth more than free Starbucks for life.

***

"Shit!" The bookend fell from Mallory's hand while we hovered in front of Tommy's body. "What did I do?"

Archie sighed. "Don't apologize. Chad would be dead if it wasn't for your quick thinking."

"That doesn't mean Tommy deserved to die," Mallory said. "We were only supposed to rough him up."

Wow. For once, I hadn't shuddered from something Mallory said. Her contradiction—despising Tommy one minute and then whimpering about his death the next—provided a small comfort. Perhaps she had a shred of humanity left and could become a better person. Most people wouldn't worry about the person who tried to kill their best friend or turned their life into a nightmare.

"It was self-defense," Archie said.

"I can't do this right now!" Mallory exclaimed.

She darted through the living room. The deck door slammed shut after another beat, creating an echo.

Archie's jaw twitched. "I should check on her—make sure she doesn't do anything stupid."

"Good idea."

Yeah. I meant what I said. Petty jealously would've only made life more complicated. We needed to be aware of Mallory no matter how much rage shot through my body from Archie and Mallory having alone time. One wrong move, and we'd be in jail.

I turned my head.

Archie could've been the Flash, because he left before I could blink. Whatever. The sooner he dealt with Mallory, the sooner we could spin our story.

I continued surveying Tommy's body. More specifically, the dried blood on his forehead. No matter how much I always anticipated the universe's surprises, I couldn't stop scoffing. One moment my former childhood best friend was alive and the next he was dead. There was just something final about death that I shouldn't have had to deal with so early in life. Especially when his earlier vague comments were the closest thing I had to closure. That one summer afternoon tryst was the only thing I had to remember him by.

The door clinked, and I jerked my body around.

Kelly couldn't have been home—it was only a little before eight and the Snowflake Ball wasn't over till eleven.

The clinking continued and my heart fluttered. I had to do something fast if I didn't wanna be caught. I couldn't check up on Mallory and Archie—not yet. Being around Mallory during one of her emotional moments was less fun than chemistry homework.

The door started opening, and I did the only thing I could. I hid against the den wall before the turn in the hallway.

My pulse hadn't stopped vibrating in my ears despite me counting to twenty in my head. If even a small chance existed that Kelly would discover what Mallory, Archie, and I did, then I'd need sedatives for the rest of my life.

I peeked outward from the den.

Kelly's hand remained clapped over her mouth while she stood in front of Tommy. Then, she scratched her head. "What the hell?" she bellowed.

Shit. Shit. Shit. There was no returning to a normal life. Kelly would uncover the truth in a matter of seconds, and Mallory, Archie, and I were doomed. It wasn't like Kelly and Mallory were best friends, and she'd exert herself for her younger sister.

No matter how much my heart should've shattered from anticipating what would happen, nothing could've prepared me for what occurred next. Not a film, television show, self-help book, pamphlet, or therapist.

Tommy grunted before rubbing his eyes. "Those assholes have a lot of nerve."

Good gracious. Tommy couldn't have been alive—Mallory hit him pretty good, and that should've ended the Tommy problem.

Kelly kneeled. "What do we have here?"

"Please." Tommy looked upward, struggling to take a breath. "You've gotta help me—I need to get checked out by a doctor."

"What are you doing here?" Kelly asked. "The whole town thought you were missing."

"It's your bitch of a sister," Tommy said. "She tried to kill me, and you've gotta help me—I beg you."

Kelly scoffed. "I don't care what you want. You were never good enough for Mallory, and I'm gonna end you."

"What the hell are you talking about?" Tommy asked.

"It's simple. I'm gonna do what Mallory couldn't."

"Huh?"

"Have fun in Hell, asshole." In one swift motion, Kelly snatched the bookend—which was a few inches from Tommy's head. She repeatedly smashed it against his forehead, blood gushing down Tommy's body.

I covered my mouth, muffling my screams. No matter how despicable Tommy was, I hadn't wanted him to die. Yikes. Any negative opinion I had of Mallory didn't compare to Kelly. She actually did it. She killed Tommy—not Mallory.

"Well?" Kelly snapped, dragging me from my digression.

"You killed Tommy, not Mallory," I said.

She cackled. "I've got no idea what you're talking about."

"Don't play dumb. You grabbed the bookend and bashed it against his face over and over again."

Yeah. Time to get to the point. Kelly hadn't done herself any favors by denying the truth. She was only wasting my time, and I couldn't have that. Mom's sleeping pill could wear off at a moment's notice, and I couldn't have her wondering where I was. If she became involved with the Tommy situation—then that added another variable. And it was a complication I couldn't have. My reasoning was practically an unwritten law of physics—the chances of a problem becoming worse increased with each subsequent person who discovered the truth.

"Fine," she said. "You're right. I killed Tommy, because there was no way Mallory would survive the scandal."

"Why help her after all your animosity?" I asked.

Kelly placed her hands in her lap. "Haven't you been paying attention? She's my only family."

"Do we understand each other?"

"What you and Gemma did sucks."

"You gave me Mallory's locker combination," I said.

Yeah. If Kelly tried making me feel guilty, then I'd do the same to her. She had no moral standing in this situation, and she needed to be reminded of that fact ASAP. Hypocrisy was about as low as people got. I might not have been perfect, yet I had no problem owning up to what I did to Mallory in front of Kelly.

"Doesn't mean I like it—I did what I thought was right," Kelly said.

"Should've thought about that earlier," I said.

Kelly's eyebrows inched upward. "What happened to you?"

"Mallory happened. Anyway, it's kind of odd you wanna set Mallory free, yet not take responsibility for your actions."

"Have you forgotten all this startled because you wouldn't leave Archie and Mallory alone?"

I groaned. "God. You sound just like your sister. What you two don't realize is Tommy still had a gun on him."

"You better not hold this over my head for the rest of my life."

"Relax. I only want my happy ending with Archie," I said.

"You're too young to worry about that."

"I'll take my chances," I said.

"You should be ashamed of yourself. Sending your best friend away is horrendous."

"I'm doing what I have to do. Besides, she's in a sanitarium—not prison. So, she'll be fine."

"How do you live with yourself?" Kelly demanded.

"I've already addressed that."

She bit her lip. "If you're willing to blame Mallory for a crime she didn't commit, then you can't be too secure in your love for Archie."

Please. It'd take more than Kelly's tough love to rattle me. She didn't have a right to judge me, so I wouldn't sweat her comment. Not when the euphoria from my happy ending with Archie surpassed any high from a drug.

"Have you forgotten about that other thing in your safe?" I asked.

"My curiosity doesn't mean she's guilty of killing those other boys."

"You saved the articles."

"It was just something to consider."

"We're done." I opened the car door without another word. The wind picked up, yet the breeze resembled the warmth from before—there wasn't a hint of iciness to it. Then, I strutted up my driveway.

Just because I reached my limit of arguing with Kelly didn't mean I stopped contemplating the issue. I did what needed to be done, and I wouldn't apologize for my behavior—I hadn't physically harmed Mallory. Morality was also elastic. Doing the right thing sometimes meant doing the socially unacceptable thing. If roles were reversed, then Mallory would've betrayed me. In fact, she already had with pursuing Archie after my first conversation with him in addition to her indecent proposal.

FRIDAY, APRIL 5, 2019

I smirked upon entering a room after school.

"How did you get in here?" Mallory adjusted her white gown while remaining in bed. "I'm not allowed visitors."

"Said I was your cousin and bribed a nurse."

"I should've known you'd stop by."

"I had to see you for myself," I said.

"What do you want?" Mallory asked.

"Thought it'd be fun to reminisce with an old friend."

Mallory grunted. "Enough bullshit—I know you didn't visit me to catch up."

"You're right."

"Say whatever you came to say, then leave, because you've got some nerve showing up here. Giving me the money was all you had to do, and we could've been done with each other. But no. You called the cops."

Mallory should've been more careful. Bitterness wasn't a flattering emotion on her—it only reminded me of the worst side of her. Like the Mallory who didn't have a problem with pursuing Archie for revenge or concocting an indecent proposal on a whim.

"You didn't snitch on Archie, Rebecca, Dan, and me to the police," I said.

"I'm not clueless—there's no way for me to prove your culpability in Tommy's death. I'd also rather handle you myself."

"How astute of you."

Mallory hissed. "Just go. You aren't wanted here."

"Planting your diary, the gun, and flash drive in your locker is the least of your problems."

"What are you getting at?"

"You didn't kill Tommy."

"Maybe you should join me here—you don't seem to be remembering things correctly."

Please. I wouldn't have wanted to chat with Mallory if she were the last person on Earth after I finished gloating. No thanks. I had better things to do. Like wondering what colleges were worth applying to, planning dates with Archie, and working on my short stories.

"You ran out to the woods and Archie chased after you," I revealed.

"So?"

"And you know Kelly left the dance super early because of a migraine, but that isn't the whole story."

"I don't have time for this," Mallory said.

No need for Mallory's overreaction. She didn't have anything better to do—that was the advantage of being tossed away and forgotten about in a sanitarium.

I let out a faint laugh. "Tommy was still alive after you hit him with the bookend."

"Impossible."

"I wasn't outside in your backyard before I checked on you and Archie," I said. "I was hiding against your den wall and saw Kelly hit Tommy with the bookend over and over again."

"I don't believe you; Kelly despises me," Mallory said.

"She's still your sister."

She quirked her eyebrows. "Why tell me?"

"The only thing worse than your best friend setting you up for a crime you committed is being locked up for a crime you didn't commit."

Yeah. The contempt radiating from her face was worth more than an acceptance from Columbia or Brown. For once, she understood what being helpless felt like. And maybe, just maybe, she'd become a better person someday. If she remembered the disgust that must've been oozing from her right now, then she might be less likely to get revenge or concoct an indecent proposal in the future.

Her eyes bulged more. "Are you kidding?"

"Nope. I finally got revenge—guess you shouldn't have underestimated me."

"Do you hate me that much?"

"You should know better than to ask that question," I said.

Mallory started panting. "I was trying to become a better person by going to counseling."

"That was an act."

"Not this time."

"Doesn't matter. I know better than to believe you," I said.

An acrid sent burned my nostrils. Didn't know how I hadn't noticed the odor before—cleaning product had a distinct aroma, and Mallory's room must've been cleaned right before I arrived.

"You should be ashamed of yourself," Mallory said.

"I did what I had to do, and Archie and I are gonna be so happy now."

"I could kill you right here and get away with it—my life can't get any worse; I'm already locked away."

"Even you aren't that clueless."

Mallory blinked. "No?"

"You just revealed you wanna deal with me yourself."

"Maybe killing you right here and right now is my way of handling you," she said.

"You're still guilty of other things even if you didn't kill Tommy."

"I'm not sure what you're getting at."

I clenched my teeth. "I know about Parker and Jordon. Parker allegedly drowned in his indoor hot tub while Jordon supposedly drowned in his pool. Yet they both played sports. And you can't forget about the similarities. Parker cheated on you and Jordon cheated on Sami—your pal from the debate team. Seems like you've got a problem with guys who can't be faithful. First Parker and Jordon and then Tommy."

"Doesn't ring a bell."

"Maybe you've blacked out the events because you can't cope with the guilt," I said.

"Okay. Let's say you're correct—you can't prove anything."

"You're right; I can't. But you owe me honesty since I confessed everything to you."

She shrugged. "Fine, I killed Parker and Jordon. Happy?"

"Hardly."

Yeah. My previous low opinion of Mallory didn't compare to the one forming in my head. Mallory's culpability with Jordon and Parker dying meant she was more depraved than I ever imagined. And said fact probably meant staring at my bedroom ceiling longer each night. Cheating didn't mean Parker and Jordon deserved to die.

"Leave," Mallory spat. "I can't stand the sight of you."

My smirk intensified. "Not yet. I deserve a few more minutes of gloating."

"You defeated me, so there's no reason for your continued bragging."

"I'm not done yet."

"What are you babbling about?"

"There's something you should know about our threesome," I said.

She shrilled at me. "I don't wanna listen to this."

"I don't really care what you want."

"Archie was all I thought about it when it was our turn during the threesome. And I only slept with you because I didn't wanna lose Archie in addition to how I couldn't alienate you while I schemed with Gemma."

Yeah. This conversation was better than the anticipation of opening presents on Christmas morning. She finally got what was coming to her, and my only regret was how this moment wouldn't last forever. Mallory deserved a lifetime of misery after all of her misdeeds.

"You're a prick," Mallory said.

I gave her a mock frown. "Ouch. My feelings are hurt."

"I'm gonna scream if you don't leave in the next five seconds."

"You wanna know something?" I picked at my nail, peeling the excess white part off. "Sleeping with you was the worst ten minutes of my life, and I'll never get that time back."

"This ends right now." Mallory screamed before jumping out of her bed. She rushed over to me, my head banging against the wall. Her hands traveled from my shoulders to my neck while I tried catching my breath. Her grip was so tight that it felt like my windpipe would be crushed any second—like an elephant sat on my throat. No matter how much I budged, I couldn't shove Mallory off me.

So, yeah. Probably a matter of seconds before my life flashed before my eyes.

Footsteps shuffled against the ground before two men in white scrubs burst into the room.

"What's going on?" asked a bald man.

They pushed Mallory off me in a matter of seconds, yet my breathing didn't slow down. If anything, my pulse soared faster.

"What are you doing here?" asked the redhead. "Mallory isn't allowed visitors.

"Doesn't matter—I was leaving anyway."

I exited the room and scurried through the hallway towards the elevator.

Wow. I couldn't believe how close I came to death. No amount of hubris was worth dying for, and I wouldn't underestimate Mallory in the future.

I would've been lying if I didn't acknowledge my smile once I stepped into the elevator, though. My near-death experience didn't erase the satisfaction radiating through me because of Mallory knowing I wasn't weak.

Pressing the lobby button happened after another beat, and I almost drew blood from biting my lip so hard. I had to pray Mallory wouldn't be released from the sanitarium for a long time. I deserved a slight reprieve before speculating about Mallory's next move.

SATURDAY, APRIL 6, 2019

"You shouldn't have visited Mallory," Archie said.

We sat on our towels while a salty odor drifted through the air and waves crashed into the sand in the distance. The first Saturday in April was the perfect opportunity for a beach outing—important to appreciate the good weather while we could.

"I had to see her," I said.

Archie sighed. "Promise you won't do it again?"

"I won't."

"Fantastic." Archie ruffled my hair. "I'd hate if anything happened to you. I just got you back."

I winked. "Great to know you care."

"Is that seriously even a question?" he asked.

"Relax. I was teasing."

"I'm sorry, but I'm gonna be on edge about Mallory for the foreseeable future. I can't imagine what life will be like once she's released."

"Here's an idea. How about we don't discuss Mallory?" I asked.

He smiled. "Fine by me."

"Although I'll say one more thing."

"And what's that?"

"Thanks for not judging me for framing her," I said.

He let out a louder breath this time. "I'm not happy about it. However, I'm not gonna let my disappointment keep me from being happy. Especially because she's guilty."

My heart thumped faster for a split second. I didn't wanna consider what would happen if Archie ever realized I knew Kelly really killed Tommy, no matter how much pleasure Mallory's downfall brought me. If he discovered the truth, then he might dump me. Getting away with a second "despicable" thing pushed my luck, because the universe wasn't that kind.

So, yeah. Like everything else in life, I'd live with what I did—any guilt was fleeting. I won. Mallory lost. Game over—for now, at least.

Chris Bedell's previous publishing credits include Thought Catalog, Entropy Magazine, Chicago Literati, and Foliate Oak Literary Magazine, among others. His debut YA Fantasy novel IN THE NAME OF MAGIC was published by NineStar Press in 2018. His 2019 books include his NA Thriller BURNING BRIDGES (BLKDOG Publishing) and his YA Paranormal Romance novel DEATHLY DESIRES (Deep Hearts YA). In addition to his YA Thriller BETWEEN LOVE AND MURDER, Chris has another book releasing in 2020. His YA Contemporary I'LL SEE YOU AGAIN (Deep Hearts YA). Furthermore, Chris graduated with a BA in Creative Writing from Fairleigh Dickinson University in 2016.